Cracking Grace

A short novel

Stephen Stromp

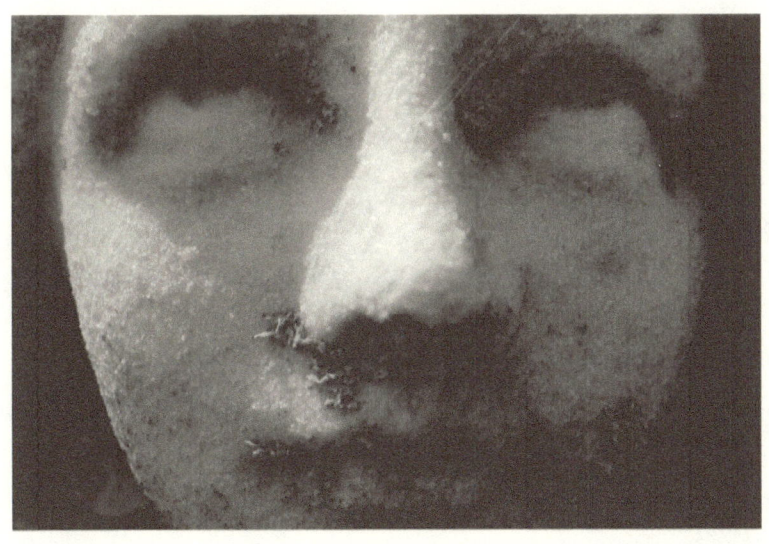

W.O.P. Press

Cracking Grace

Copyright © 2006, 2014 by Stephen Stromp. All rights reserved.

Cover photography, interior photographs and chalk drawing by Shawn DuBois. Cover design by Stephen Stromp.

Epitaph written in 1889 by Pearl Starr for her mother, Belle Starr.

The Worms Crawl In is a traditional folksong originating from the 19th century.

ISBN-13: 978-0615970653

ISBN-10: 0615970656

Published by W.O.P Press

10 9 8 7 6 5 4 3 2

Shed not for her the bitter tear
Nor give the heart to vain regret
'Tis but the casket that lies here
The gem that filled it sparkles yet
- 1889

Cracking Grace

1
AUDREY

Audrey sat at the kitchen table twirling her spoon in a bowl of oatmeal. She let the tasteless lumps stick to the end of the spoon as she watched the rain give a drink to the surrounding pines. Outside, her mind could wander. She could become lost in the raindrops. She could *become* their sound and liquid movement. She escaped by pretending that like them, she was liquid. Liquid, so she didn't have to think, and the only power over her was gravity.

Inside, it was colder than the week before. Even though summer was steadily approaching, a chill had permeated the house. The large home boasted two woodstoves and a fireplace, yet her father heated them only intermittently now.

It had been a magical place to live. Though on the outside the home appeared to be an enchanted log cabin nestled under gigantic pines, the interior was more like a sprawling ranch, with the main rooms converging under a massive cathedral ceiling. Beneath this centerpiece was the open living room, kitchen and dining room. Large picture windows lined both the front and backsides of the house allowing anyone inside to feel a part of the surrounding wilderness. Yet somehow, despite its openness, it managed to be cozy. Audrey imagined the three of them joined together in a secret adventure away from civilization.

But it wasn't just the house that made it magical. Audrey's mother placed great importance on creativity and the arts. She said it ran in the family. There were always projects: painting, making puppets out of socks and buttons, sculpting clay. The summer before, Audrey had taken a special interest in making short movies. Her mother encouraged her to use the family video camera whenever she wished and would often help her with the scripts. But Audrey insisted on doing the filming herself. She didn't want any surprises revealed before her premiers, which were complete with one-dollar admission tickets and popcorn.

In several of her mini-movies, Audrey played the character of detective Anne Meadows. *The Case of the Missing Jewels* was her favorite. The living room, with its vaulted ceiling, was easily converted into the interior of a castle where the medieval story took place. In it, Anne Meadows was commissioned by an evil queen (also played by herself) to help recover her stolen jewels. When she solved the case and returned the jewels, the evil queen then turned on her. It was all quite dramatic, ending with a climactic battle scene in the forest. For the queen's demise, an old mannequin was decapitated with a branch. Her parents gave it rave reviews. Her father claimed he was on the edge of his seat the entire time, and described the movie as "intense, yet poetic."

The house, however, was no longer her imaginary castle. Her creative inspiration had faded. She couldn't make herself look at the uninviting rooms and dim decor. She stared instead at the rain, and at the lone bluebird looking in from under the awning. She could remember only one other time she had seen a bluebird. She had been walking through the woods with her mother, who told her she'd probably never see another one because of how rare they were in Michigan.

"Audrey." Her father brushed her light brown hair from her face, bringing her back into the room. She looked back to the lumpy oatmeal; her mother's oatmeal never had any lumps. "Audrey, you know before this happened, your mother transferred some of the love she had for you to me—just so I could love you even more. I love you so much." He gave her a hug.

She appreciated his efforts, but knew his words of comfort were nothing more than words. Words could not bring her back. Words could not replace the times she modeled her mother's clothes in their own private fashion shows; they could not bring back their bike trips to the ice cream parlor where they put a piece of candy corn at the bottom of each sugar cone to keep it from leaking. She didn't want to do those things with her father. Those were traditions reserved for her and her mother.

Sure, she enjoyed separate traditions with her father. In the summer, her mother would pack them lunches, and the two would take off down the trail through the woods. When they'd get to the cemetery, she'd make him hold her hand until they crossed to the other side where the trail continued. And there, along the river, they'd enjoy a picnic. They would throw rocks in the water while he would often describe for her the surfaces of other planets. She loved to hear about other worlds. It made her think about their surroundings—about how strange the site of the colossal pines and the power lines that stretched across the river would be to an alien landing on earth for the first time. Her father had the ability to give her new perspectives.

Sadly, she predicted those picnics would stop. She feared they would no longer be able to simply pass through the cemetery. She feared the cemetery would become an insurmountable barrier keeping them from the river. How could they ever again indulge in a picnic knowing her grave sat just beyond the trees?

Slowly, she lifted her head. He had become so slim. It was clear he hadn't been eating much either. She looked into his dark eyes, which matched his dark hair. "It's been a week," she whispered.

"I know, sweetheart." He seated himself at the other end of the long oak table, so far away. She wondered why he hadn't yet removed the extra leaf after the small reception. "I can't imagine what this does to a ten-year-old," he whispered. She could tell by the way he wrinkled his forehead that he was concentrating, that he was concerned with choosing the right words to say to her. He placed his hand over his eyes and rubbed them. "I love your mom," he said finally. "I want you to know that. I don't want you to think if I don't show emotion or—"

"I know you miss her, dad," she stopped him. Audrey wasn't concerned that he lacked signs of mourning. She *expected* his feelings to be buried in the beginning. Buried, for her. Even during the funeral, his face was stone, unmoving. She suspected he would deal with her death at a later time, after he was sure *she* was alright.

"I'm not really hungry," she said. He kept his eyes closed and folded his hands before him. She wondered if he was praying, although she hadn't seen him pray before. She didn't want to leave him alone, yet she could not bear to stay. She left her cold oatmeal on the table and started for her room.

There, she sat on the edge of her bed, assuming a new angle on the forest through the giant window. The surrounding pines, which at one time had given her a sense of comfort, now seemed to close in around the house. They blocked out the sunlight, plentiful in summers before. *She* made everything light. Without her, they seemed trapped together in an enveloping darkness.

Audrey was startled as the bluebird she had seen from the dining room flew into her view and landed on the sill outside her window. She was ready to call her mother in to show her its beautiful, rare feathers—when she remembered. She stood from her bed and caressed the bird on the other side of the glass, as if she were stroking his feathers with her finger. He gazed inside, not flinching until she drew back her hand. He then flew between the pines and through the drops of rain towards the stone outline of the crypt in the distance.

Audrey would only enter the cemetery when she was with her mother or father. She didn't mind bringing snacks to her father while he was mowing or planting; and she didn't mind helping him weed or rake—just as long as he stayed in plain view.

Only once did she wander alone into the clearing. She had become lost in the woods while collecting acorns and pinecones for a wreath she and her mother planned on making. Her body froze as she encountered the headstones and statues. She stood still for a full ten minutes working up the nerve to move her legs again. She tried to convince herself that she could be brave as long as it was daytime. Light, she reasoned, kept everything frightening away.

When she finally found the strength to move, her curiosity brought her to the aboveground crypt of Loretta Grant. It drew attention to itself being the only crypt in the cemetery. The extravagant tomb was guarded by two identical gargoyles. Each had the face of a puma or panther, had horns instead of ears, teeth as long as a saber-toothed tiger's, and eyes similar to the piercing pupils of a housecat. They were mounted on an angle, head-down, on opposite sides of the thick door, looking as if they would not hesitate to pounce on anyone who dared enter the tomb.

Audrey attempted to keep her mind off the twisted creatures as she approached. She stood on her tiptoes, stretching to catch a glimpse inside the tiny square window near the top of the door. Yet it was not through the window where her curiosity was fulfilled. Out of the corner of her eye, she saw movement—flowing purple. Slowly, she turned to see an old woman floating past, her feet not touching the ground. Her white hair flowed wildly as if she were underwater. She wore a pearl necklace and large rings on every finger, but it was her purple dress waving behind her that forever stuck with Audrey. The woman did not look at her, nor did she speak. It was as if she only wanted to make herself known. Still, Audrey found herself unable to move in her presence. The woman circled the crypt before disappearing into the trees on the other side of the clearing. Only then were Audrey's legs finally unglued; and they wasted no time carrying her swiftly back through the forest.

Her father nearly fell off his ladder while adjusting the floodlights as Audrey ran into the yard yelling. She swore she had seen the ghost of Loretta Grant, but he immediately dismissed it, blaming her vivid imagination on the apparition. "Just look at your movies!" he told her with a grin. "A young lady *that* creative is bound to have her mind play tricks on her from time to time." With that response, she learned to never speak again about what she had seen. And the experience was enough to keep her from becoming lost in the forest ever again.

Her parents had moved to the small town of Ruthsford shortly before Audrey was born. And before her father became the caretaker, its cemetery had been in ruins. Teens with little to occupy their time found a favorite pastime in vandalizing the site. Gravestones had been toppled, graffiti covered Loretta Grant's crypt, and the grounds were overgrown and littered with trash.

Her father took it upon himself to make sure the resting souls received the peace and respect they deserved. He repaired the gravestones; cleaned and landscaped the grounds; he posted signs stating only family and loved ones were allowed to enter; he even patrolled most nights with a flashlight before going to bed, making sure no one was disturbing the site. He was proud, proud to maintain the monuments as well as the land's natural beauty. But most of all, he was proud of the new additions he had given the cemetery.

Besides being the caretaker, he was also an amazing sculptor and stone carver. People came from all over Michigan to purchase a statue he created for their lawn, garden, memorial or gravesite. But he took special pride in the statues he created for the Ruthsford cemetery. Of course, there were the gargoyles that had been commissioned as additions to Loretta Grant's crypt, but he created two others that had not been commissioned by anyone. He made them as a gift to the land—and as a gift to those buried beneath it. He had once said there was a part of him in both statues. The statue of the Virgin Mary, positioned in the middle of the graves, he explained, represented his respectful and compassionate side; while the statue of Jesus, upon the hill overlooking the cemetery, represented his watchful eye and his important role as a father. Her mother agreed that the statue portrayed Jesus in a more tender form than ever before, with his open arms embracing the land below and all the souls who passed through it.

To Audrey, however, Jesus looked menacing. She could not see his loving embrace. To her, his open arms looked like he *dominated* the land—everything above and under it. Even Mary, with her solemn face, unsettled Audrey. Like Jesus, her arms were also open, her unswaying robe draped from her elbows. She looked to be eternally awaiting a hug. Audrey often wondered if she *was* to grant her the anticipated hug, would the stone arms close in around her, suffocate, and ultimately crush her? And their eyes—she could feel them watching her whenever she was in the cemetery. She suspected they spied on her and her parents. She even imagined they listened to their conversations. Audrey kept these thoughts to herself, of course. She knew her father would be heartbroken if he knew.

Audrey lay back on her bed and closed her eyes. She began to hum, then to sing. She thought she had forgotten the words that came flooding back to her, the song her mother had taught her. They would sing it together on days there was a burial to keep from dwelling on the somberness of death—to turn the seriousness of it into silliness. She sang to the ceiling in a light whisper:

> *Didja ever think as a hearse goes by*
> *That you might be the next to die?*
> *They wrap you up in a big white sheet*
> *And bury you down six feet deep.*

They put you in a big black box
And cover you up with dirt and rocks.
All goes weak for about a week,
And then the coffin begins to leak!

The worms crawl in, the worms crawl out;
The worms play pinochle on your snout;
They eat your eyes, they eat your nose;
They eat the jelly between your toes.

Then a great big worm with rolling eyes
Crawls in your stomach and out your eyes.
Your insides turn slimy green,
And pus pours out like whipping cream!

Audrey thought of graves. She thought of worms. She imagined them playing pinochle on her mother's nose. The thought disgusted her. After her mother's death, she didn't know what to think of the bodies in the cemetery. In her head, she had always referred to the statues, Loretta Grant's ghost and the bodies beneath—as *them*. It was a different world. But now, her mother had become a part of it. She was in a place that Audrey didn't understand; and she didn't find much comfort in the idea that the statues watched over her. In fact, she hated the cemetery for holding her mother captive—for keeping her in that world. She wanted only to be away from it, the woods, and the cold house.

She pulled herself off her bed and searched the house for her father. She found him in the office and knocked lightly on the half open door. He spun around in the chair, giving her a smile. "I was just doing some work on the computer," he said, but Audrey could see over his shoulder that the screen was blank. "What's up?"

"I was thinking. Why couldn't we let someone else watch over the cemetery for the summer?"

"Why would we want to do that, honey?"

"I thought that maybe we could get away from here. You know, a break from the cemetery would do you good."

"Well thanks for the offer, Audrey," he said with a light chuckle. "But I'm sure I'll do just fine. *We'll* do just fine. Besides, who else is going to look after Mom?"

"The priest said *God* will."

He bent forward and reached for Audrey. He held her chin tightly and looked into her eyes. "As long as your mother is out there, *I'm* going to watch over her," he said with determination. "Do you understand, Audrey? And I want you to be my helper. Can you do that for me, honey?"

"Yes," she agreed softly before heading back to watch the rain.

2
MARY

Mary had the best view. Even so, the others could only wonder why she never tired of the rolling treeless landscape that plummeted to the river. But to Mary, it didn't matter that her position was unchanging. She was able to observe constant movement, the constant changes that took place all around her: the leaves across the river, their changing season after season from dark green to reds and oranges and then falling to the earth; the rainbows; the sunsets; the dark and vast, vibrant blue, and pink-hued skies; the foggy mists; the frozen grass poking through thin layers of snow; the melting ice along the edges of the river each spring. All of this gave her a sense of wonderment and intrigue. Even though she was unable to participate, even though she was a mere spectator of the world that surrounded her, she was nonetheless in awe of this ever-changing *life*.

The only indications of what century it was were the power lines that stretched across the river and the dates on the most recent markers near the bank. The setting would've been a dream for picnic goers if it wasn't hidden deep in the forest, the only entrance being a thinly-etched two-track off a secondary road.

Mary wished more people would visit her. How she loved when children would visit! They came not as often as she desired though. Children were such a pleasant reminder of what was exciting about the world. They reminded her of herself. If she were freed from her platform, like them, she too would have explored the monuments with curiosity. Their playfulness down by the river brightened up the sorrowful thoughts put in her head by the mourners. Unlike the children, she would often dread when *they* came to see her. They came to cry and pour their misery out to her ears, recalling details of their loved one's life—and unjust demise. Memorable moments shared with parents, sisters, brothers, and lovers were told to Mary. "Why?" they would often ask her. "Why Mama? Or Timmy? Or Josephine? *Why?*" But Mary offered no answer. Her unchanging face could only stare back at them in sympathy. She had no answers for the grieving.

Rain and wind pelted her figure. She loved the rain because it cleaned her; she never felt the chill of the pulsating water. And she didn't know how hard the wind was blowing (or if it blew at all) unless she noticed movement of the trees and power lines. The mourners, she figured, were like the wind. If she closed her eyes and ears forever, she would never be aware of the sorrow they brought to her. She never *had* to watch the mourners become old until they too became part of the land. Yet along with the others, she kept her inside eyes open. She took in as much as possible, capturing the events surrounding her because she knew even if she couldn't see or feel it, the wind was still there, affecting her just the same.

Bluebell shot out of the trees like a blue dart. He flew past Mary and dodged some of the higher markers in front of her. "You're such a beautiful bluebird, Bluebell," she told him. He would frequently fly for her, entertaining her. "Fly in front of me again so I can see you!" He flew in a circle around her head before landing on her shoulder. There, he sat proud. He would sit there all day if she asked, but most nights were too cold for him; he slept in his home along the wooded path. The rain was chilly, but he promised Mary he'd keep an eye on them. If he didn't, he knew she'd worry all day.

"How are they doing?" she asked.

"It's hard to say, Mary. I suppose they're doing as well as expected."

Bluebell was more than her best friend. He was her link, collecting information for her on events that took place beyond her sight. Because of him, Mary's eyes were not limited to her view of the river. In a sense, wherever Bluebell went, Mary went too. Whatever he saw, so did she. Because of him, she was beginning to experience, learn and form opinions about things she had herself never seen.

After discovering tools and blocks of stone inside the shed, and after seeing Mr. Lansly help visitors load small statues and monuments into their vehicles, Bluebell was the one who confirmed that she and the others likely had been created by Mr. Lansly. Bluebell was also the one who told her when Mrs. Lansly had gotten sick and was too weak to get out of bed.

She was such a caring woman. Mary admired how she looked after little Audrey, and how she would help her husband pull weeds and plant flowers in the spring. Her burial had been the saddest day in the cemetery. It was especially difficult for Mary, as she was buried directly in front of her base. When Mrs. Lansly died, it was the closest Mary ever felt to becoming a mourner, to losing someone who meant something to her. At first, she didn't even necessarily *feel* grief. She didn't know that emotion. She only knew from the mourners how she was *supposed* to feel. But soon, she began to develop the very emotion she witnessed; she *learned* how to feel it.

It had been a week, and Mary was still concerned for her caretaker and his daughter. She didn't care if Mr. Lansly or Audrey weren't aware of her presence. Even if they weren't being counted, she felt she owed her condolences just the same.

A strong gust grabbed hold of Bluebell and sent him flying. He tumbled into a nearby stone marker and dizzily hopped in a circle. "Stand on my other shoulder so I can guard you from the wind!" Bluebell did as Mary suggested. He always did.

"What did you hear at the church today?" she asked. He took off recklessly, suddenly remembering his most important find. He flew towards the river, chirping excitedly. The strong wind made his return flight unsteady. "What's gotten into you, Bluebell? You let that wind blow you around, it may push you right into the power lines, and you'll end up being electrocuted. Then what would I do!"

Bluebell sang out a laugh as he returned to her shoulder, not realizing how serious she was. "Birds sit on them all the time. I've never seen a bird electrocuted from sitting on a power line!"

Mary gazed up to the two lines that came out of the trees and stretched across the river. "Gerald Lee was killed by a power line. Poor Mrs. Lee told me in tears."

Bluebell flew to Gerald Lee's headstone. He balanced himself in the wind to stay atop it. "It's different for humans, Mary."

"How?"

"I don't know. It just is. Forget about it, Mary. I promise I won't fly around like that anymore. Now don't you want to hear what I found out?"

"Yes, of course!"

Mary's hunger for knowledge of the outside world was increasing with each year. She wanted to discover the meaning behind why she existed—and why she existed in that form. Why was she a statue and Bluebell a bird? Why were the Lanslys human? These were the types of conversations she would initiate with the others.

Then one day, Bluebell made a curious discovery. Inside Ruthsford's town church, he saw another statue that appeared very similar to Mary. This baffled them both. *Where did she come from? Why did they look alike?* And more importantly, *what information did this other Mary hold?* She was inside, integrated with humans. Surely she must hold the answers Mary sought!

Ever since this discovery, Mary had been constantly sending Bluebell to the church. Unable to find a way inside, he'd perch outside the windows and strain to listen to the Strange Man who spoke to the crowd. He rarely felt he overheard anything of much importance. Most of what he brought back were mysterious songs and words. They were like codes neither could decipher. "Hail Mary, full of grace. The Lord is with thee!" he chirped as he flew into the clearing one day. The words intrigued Mary, but offered her little. Even so, she whispered the mysterious poem to herself from time to time in case it might mean something to her later. She often wondered *who was Mary?* Surely it wasn't her. There were lots of Marys, some even buried in the cemetery.

Although much of what Bluebell brought back was incomprehensible, he *did* manage to accumulate a bit of useful information. Through Bluebell, Mary learned the thing that lived inside every human was called a *soul*. She figured a soul was what also lived inside her, as well as the other statues and the animals in the forest. Though she couldn't be certain, she wondered if perhaps even the trees, the plants and the river also had a soul. She learned too about heaven, a glorious place beyond the sky; and of hell, a terrible place of eternal fire.

Still, it all seemed so distant, unfathomable. It was as if the church only provided them a few pieces of a giant puzzle. Despite their frustration, Mary insisted Bluebell keep attending the meetings. If only he could somehow find his way inside, she was convinced the other Mary could help reveal the truth.

Bluebell edged his way close to Mary's neck, excited to provide her with his latest information. "The Strange Man talked about you again today!" he boasted.

"Bluebell, I doubt he was talking about me. Most of the humans that attend the meetings don't even know who I am! I only see them if one of them dies."

Bluebell pecked off a wet leaf that had flown from the oak tree and stuck to her face. "But they *must* know who you are. He spoke of—'the Virgin Mary!'"

Mary was used to that name. Sure enough, it was what the mourners would sometimes call her. Her excitement grew. Had Bluebell finally uncovered some meaning behind her existence? "What did he say! What have you learned!"

"That you're very important, Mary. You don't realize how important you are!"

"*Important?*"

"Yes. Almost as important as God!"

"But who's God?" Mary asked to no one in particular.

She knew neither Bluebell nor her had that answer. They commonly heard the word *God* used in many of the speeches given by the Strange Man. Still, neither of them knew who this person was, or even if it was a person at all. The name came to mean some sort of ruler to them, like a king. "Kingdom of God," Bluebell would often say, repeating what he had heard. God was as distant and mysterious to Mary as she was to herself.

"God—he's the one who did this to us," a deep voice groaned.

Mary and Bluebell were startled. Jesus mostly kept to himself. It was easy for him to be excluded since he was positioned far upon the hill away from the others. So when he *did* speak, he often caused a shock. "God, *grant us mercy*," he roared in his slow, deep tone. "That's what the mourners say, when the wind is strong enough to carry their voices up to me. They say God is the one who created them, and God is the one who will destroy them. God made *them*—able to move, and he made *us*—like this. It was *his* decision."

"But what's so wrong with being us?" asked Mary. "If it was God's decision to put us here, we should be thankful. Just look around you! It's beautiful—the forest, the river! Yes, we cannot move. But we're never going to die and be buried like *them*. Like Audrey's poor mother. And if we stay here forever, it also means we will never go to hell."

"Maybe we're already there, Mary."

"No. Bluebell said there would be a lake of fire." Mary watched the raindrops hitting the river. She watched them add to the cool water, disappear, and be carried away. "A lake of fire, right Bluebell?" Bluebell nodded and chirped in agreement.

"Don't you find it peculiar that you and Bluebell are the only ones overcome with joy about being here? And what's pathetic is that he can leave anytime he wants, yet he *chooses* to stay!"

"Don't be so hard on Bluebell. If it wasn't for him, none of us would even know what a soul was."

"Ahhh. But what *is* a soul? All we know is that the humans have them, and we don't. Did that church man say anything about *us* having any souls, Bluebell?"

"No," he replied, ashamed.

"Oh Jesus! The humans probably figure there's not much to us besides stone! We have to assume what the Strange Man says applies to us as well. Maybe they just don't know it does. Go on, Bluebell," she said, not wanting to debate with Jesus any further. "What did the man say about me?"

"Well. He said you gave birth to God's son."

"A child? *God's* child!" She took a moment to relish the idea before questioning how it could possibly be. Ever since she had seen Mrs. Lansly care for Audrey, she had wanted to be a mother. She looked to the sky and felt blessed. "Where is he?" she asked anxiously. "Is it one of the children who visit? Is it a cat? Or a bird?"

Bluebell cocked his head to the towering figure on the hill behind her. "Not exactly," he said. "But he *is* close to you— closer than you think."

She looked to the bugs in the grass, to the water snake gliding across the river. Then, she saw his towering reflection in Bluebell's eye. "No!" she gasped. "It can't be!"

"The man said it clearly. 'The Virgin Mary gave birth to God's son, *Jesus*,'" affirmed Bluebell.

Mary was quiet for a moment. It didn't make any sense! Her first thought was that Bluebell had misinterpreted what the man had said. It would have been easy to do, listening on the other side of a thick window. Furthermore, she knew much of the information was likely lost in the air as he flew the distance between the church and the cemetery; a bird could only remember so much. It was true she received *all* of her information second-hand through Bluebell. Through no fault of his own, it was possible he provided her distorted facts.

Yet curiously, many of the poems from the church *did* mention the name *Mary*—and *Jesus*. Could it be that the Strange Man *was* actually speaking of *them*? Mary was in no position to discredit the church. She had always been willing to believe anything. She felt if she just kept an open mind, questions about her existence would eventually start to be answered; and her purpose would begin to fall into place. She knew she couldn't stop believing in what Bluebell told her just because the idea of being a mother to someone so opinionated, someone she couldn't even see—seemed inconceivable.

Forcing herself to be positive, Mary laughed. "I guess if I'm your mother, Jesus, you have to do what I say from now on!" she joked. Jesus only groaned. "Isn't it amazing?" she marveled.

"I'll say!" he roared. "A *virgin* having a child? A *statue* having a child? It's preposterous!"

"What's a virgin?" Mary wondered. She knew it was part of the formal name given to her by the mourners, but she never realized it meant something more than an ordinary name could mean.

Jesus let out a low, yet hearty laugh. "Oh be quiet!" scolded Mary. "Just because you know a word I don't doesn't give you the right to laugh at me!" But Jesus continued laughing uncontrollably, and above his chuckling, Mary heard low growls. She looked to the crypt just beyond the oak tree. "Wonderful," she sighed. "You've woken them!"

"Splendid! I believe they'll get a good cackle out of this one."

"They're louder than two whippoorwills," she complained.

Arthur and Gareth hung from the crypt, awaking from their slumber. The gargoyles were harmless without movement, but their words were what worried Mary.

"Mary doesn't know what a virgin is," Jesus informed them.

"*Virgin?*" asked Arthur.

"*Virgin?*" asked Gareth.

"Mary doesn't know what it means to be a virgin, Arthur."

"Or what it means to *not* be a virgin, Gareth."

"And she *never* will—because *she's* the *Virgin* Mary!"

They cackled as Jesus had predicted. "Virgin! Virgin! Virgin!" they chanted in unison, as if they couldn't stop the word from freely escaping their mouths. Mary blushed on the inside.

"Who taught you that word?" she demanded to know. "You couldn't have learned it on your own!"

"*Sheeee* did," said Arthur, his voice quivering, pretending to be afraid.

"Why would she tell everyone but me?"

"Because you're too sensitive!" replied Gareth.

"Too perfect!" said Arthur.

"You couldn't handle it!"

"And because you're a girl!"

"Well I may not know what a virgin is, but I know lots of words the both of you don't!"

"Oh yeah? Tell me one word you know that we don't!" Gareth challenged.

"Gareth and I know lots of words!" said Arthur. "We even know words that rhyme with the word *word*. Why, there's *bird*."

"And *turd!*" added Gareth.

"There's *absurd*. And *cured*."

"Wait. *Cured* doesn't rhyme with *word*. Does it, Mary?"

"Will you two be quiet? I'm trying to think!"

"Think. Wink. Drink. Blink. Stink."

Mary concentrated. She thought of the mourners. She thought of their words. She thought of the words said during Mrs. Lansly's burial. "Love!" she finally announced.

"*Love?*" questioned the gargoyles.

"*Love*," Mary affirmed. "It's what the living talk to me about the most. They talk about it to you too, Jesus, only you're too far up the hill to hear it sometimes. They *love* the people buried here."

"But what does it mean?" asked Gareth.

Mary thought. "It's not what it means, I guess. It's what you *feel*."

"A *feeling?*" asked Arthur.

"She means like *mad*. And *sad*. And *glad*. And *bad*."

"I felt sad when Mrs. Lansly died," admitted Bluebell.

"What's the difference between feeling *sad* and feeling *love?*" asked Arthur.

Mary wasn't quite sure. "Nothing, I guess."

"*Love*, my dear—is money," said a low voice, reverberating from behind the oak tree. Too many cigarettes in life had left Mrs. Grant's voice raspy in death.

"Ahhhh!" Gareth screamed in mock terror. "You've woken the corpse!"

She emerged from behind the tree, hovering just above the ground. The way her purple dress flowed around her,

Mary could never tell if she actually used her legs. "*Love*," Mrs. Grant continued, "is the most expensive burial plot in the cemetery." She sauntered up to Mary. "Do you want to know what *love* is? Well, according to my husband, it was buying me this god-awful dress for my funeral. He apparently thought *love* was having me stuck in this rag for an eternity. I gave him the best years of my life, helping him build and manage a five-star restaurant to prosperity—in *Ruthsford* nonetheless. And do you know what he gave me? I'll tell you what! A fantastic one-way ticket to a lousy cemetery stuck in the middle of the woods. And don't think I don't know where he is now—buried somewhere in the city with his second wife, no doubt. They can say I died another way, but he killed me just the same."

"But Mrs. Grant. You killed *yourself*!" Mary reminded her.

"*Killed myself?*" She seemed at first surprised at the notion, but soon, her face sagged with the realization. "Suicide. Yes," she sighed, "I guess that's what they called it." She rose to Mary's platform and brought her face before hers. Mary examined her pale skin etched with crisscrossing lines of wrinkles. "I never saw killing myself as the end of me. I just thought it would be an escape. You know, moving onto bigger and better things. Frank talked like that when he decided to expand the restaurant into a chain. It was about that time I began to think I was ready to move on and expand *myself*." She rolled her hands into tight fists and shook her head from side to side. "Ha! Some businesswoman I would've made!"

Mrs. Grant turned her back to Mary, taking a moment to regain her composure. She rotated her wrist, and a long, thin cigarette appeared between her fingers. It flickered against the morning mist, which had replaced the rain. "Do you know what he said to me one night? We slept in separate rooms, you know. He came into my room one night and he said, 'Loretta, we're going under. I'll have to sell the business at a loss next week.' He left the room with his head held so low, I almost felt sorry for him. Well, I didn't have to wait for that next week to find out what was going to happen. I already knew he wouldn't sell. I knew he'd fight tooth-and-nail for that damned restaurant before he'd give in. And sure enough, he scrounged up some investors. These crooks convinced him that with enough collateral, he could not only keep the restaurant, but expand it into a chain. Can you imagine? A seventy-five-year-old fool trying to franchise a business? I begged him to retire years earlier, but it was his true love, you see, and I knew he'd let it drag us into financial oblivion. So I thought, *why should I stick around?* I couldn't compete with The Silver Dollar restaurant when it was in business, and I knew I surely couldn't replace it after it had been destroyed by his stupidity!"

"You could've just left. You didn't have to kill yourself, Mrs. Grant," suggested Mary.

She peered back to Mary from over her shoulder. "*Leave!* Where would I have gone with this old body?" She sprung from Mary's platform and floated several feet into the air, where she twisted to once again face Mary. Upon her delicate descent, she lifted the bottom of her dress and displayed her knobby knees and pale legs covered with purple veins. "No dear, all signs pointed in the direction I chose," she said as she neared the ground. "You see, Fuzzer and Finley were the ones who kept me alive for as long as I was."

"*Fuzzer and Finley?*"

"My two cats—a *beautiful* calico and *gorgeous* tabby. They *loved* me! They were mine, something Frank didn't have control over. But as he foolishly tried to save his business, my beautiful babies both died within days of each other. Well, I had them ever since I quit working in that dull restaurant myself. And with them gone, I was certain I didn't have a thing left to live for. That's when I found a rope, marched straight into the basement and hung myself from the water pipe! My only regret is that I didn't do it thirty years sooner." She raked her bony fingers through her unkempt hair. "Now I'm stuck here forever with this dreadful wrinkled skin and ghastly white hair!"

Mary often wondered why Mrs. Grant was the only person in the cemetery who did not stay dead, why she instead had been transformed into an apparition trapped on the land with herself, Jesus and the gargoyles. She didn't dare ask Mrs. Grant her thoughts on the subject seeing as she refused to help Mary and Bluebell in their quest for understanding. She rarely attended the church meetings while living, and repeatedly claimed she didn't have any of the answers they sought.

Mrs. Grant sashayed her way back to her crypt and sat upon its stoop. She took a long drag from her cigarette and exhaled. The smoke created a cloud just above her. Arthur and Gareth began to wheeze and cough. "Would you put out your stick of stink?" Gareth complained.

"Yeah! You're killing us," coughed Arthur.

"It could be worse, Arthur. At least it covers up that rotten smell she *usually* has!"

"Don't start," Mary groaned. She closed her eyes and put an invisible hand to her forehead. Taunting Mrs. Grant was the gargoyles' specialty.

Mrs. Grant floated above the stoop until she was eye-level with the creatures. "Some protectors you two are! I feel *so* safe with you outside my door. Ha! My husband would've crushed you!"

"Oh yeah? Well we never asked to guard an old hag's dive in the first place!" Gareth quipped.

Mrs. Grant took a deep breath and brought her nose to Gareth's. She looked as if she would explode in anger, but her voice came out instead in a hushed, restrained tone. Through her clenched teeth, she said, "My body may be old, but I want you two to know long after you crumble to dust, I'll still be dancing on grave tops!" With that, she leapt atop the nearest headstone. Gracefully, she jumped from one to the next. She paused occasionally to dip backwards atop some, extending her arms elegantly behind her. Atop others, she pointed her toes like a ballerina. She performed swan dives from the highest stones; and as she neared the ground, she sauntered back and forth like a weightless feather before swiftly rising once again. All the while she sang, "la dee da da dee la dee dee."

"How beautiful, Mrs. Grant," said Mary. Bluebell agreed.

"Booo!" shouted Arthur.

"I didn't know prunes could dance!" yelled Gareth

"Pull her off the stage! Where's the hook?"

Mrs. Grant continued her dance until she faded against the backdrop of the river. Yet within the next instant, she reappeared hovering again before Arthur and Gareth. The two startled gargoyles let out a shriek. Mary couldn't help but laugh, but then quieted as Mrs. Grant took another long drag from her cigarette. The smoke from her exhale grew into a massive cloud that hovered in front of her crypt, leaving Arthur and Gareth gasping. When the cloud finally dissipated, Mrs. Grant was nowhere to be found. She did not reappear for the rest of the day.

And so the day was usual for Mary—with Bluebell on her shoulder; with Jesus sharing his cynical comments, challenging her views; with the gargoyles, Arthur and Gareth, providing embarrassment for Mary and frustration for Mrs. Grant, who thought nothing more of her situation than another blame for her husband to take. In the center of the cemetery—in the center of it all, was Mary. She wasn't sure if she was in heaven. She wasn't sure if she was in hell. She wasn't sure of anything concerning her existence except that she was in the center, in the middle of *something*.

3
THE RIVER

"There's a flood watch for Ottawa County," her father declared. "That's us!" He grabbed the small radio from across the table and pulled it close to his head.

The beginning of June had crept away. The constant rain and drizzle turned the forest a rich, dark green. The day, it seemed, was as dark as night at times. The wet leaves of the nearby ash, oak, and maple trees began to weigh on their branches. They hung low in the yard. They blocked the usual walking paths as if they were attempting to keep the pair ever more isolated. Audrey kept track of her days solely by her periods of sleep. She dreamt of September, when she could go back to school. She wanted nothing more than to be out of the dimness. She wanted to be with other children. But unlike past summers, her school friends hadn't even called to play. They were afraid, she reasoned. Afraid of death, afraid of how fragile they'd have to treat her. She was tempted to call them, but she felt an obligation to her father. She had become his lone follower.

Audrey attempted to replicate her mother's routine. He never told her she had to, but she made sure the laundry was done, the dishes were washed and the beds were made. She took it upon herself to make breakfast, while letting him take care of dinner. She realized she wasn't as good as her mother at any of these things. Their clothes were wrinkled. The ends of their sheets hung out from beneath their comforters. And the most edible breakfast she could come up with were pancakes made from a pre-mixed batter that required she only add water and shake the mix in a plastic jug.

She poured him his morning orange juice. "If that river gets any higher, we'll have to start stacking sandbags. We can't risk a flooded cemetery." He pushed back his chair and opened a high cupboard only he could reach. He pulled out a glass bottle filled with something that was clear like water, but Audrey knew it wasn't. He drank half the orange juice and then poured in the liquid, filling the glass again. She placed her dishes in the sink and began to head for her room when he called after her. "Don't forget, we're having lunch with your mother today."

"But it's raining like crazy!"

"That's right!" he scolded her. "How would you like to be left alone in the pouring rain?"

"I wouldn't dad," she agreed, ashamed.

She reappeared from her room just before lunch, in time to make a peanut butter and jelly sandwich for herself and a cheese and mayonnaise sandwich for him. She finished just as he came in from the side door wearing a black rain slicker. She quickly shoved the sandwiches into a paper sack. She didn't have a raincoat, so she put on her green winter coat and tennis shoes. Together, they trudged down the muddy path, each holding a giant umbrella and camping chair. They sat their chairs beneath the outstretched limbs of the large oak tree near her grave—beneath the towering statue of Mary.

"How are you doing, honey?" he asked the gravestone.

Audrey let him do the talking. She didn't know what to say. In fact, their lunch dates with her mother made her uneasy. She saw little use in them. A stone marker and a faint outline where the ground had been sliced into over a month ago were not proper replacements for her mother. And if her mother *could* actually hear them, she was convinced they didn't need to be standing over her coffin for their words to reach her. She entertained her father's wishes, of course, but part of her couldn't help but feel foolish. She looked up to Mary. Her solemn smile seemed to mock them as they carried on the futile charade.

"Marcy called last night. Remember her from college? She wanted to tell us that her and Mark are having their summer pool party on July 20th. She asked how you were. I guess she hadn't heard, so I told her you were doing just fine. I simply said you were in the cemetery when she asked to talk with you. Don't worry about the business. We met our goal again for the spring. The Patterson's missed another payment, but I called them last night. They said the check is on its way. Audrey's report card came." He rubbed her shoulder. "She did as perfect as always. She made the most delicious pancakes for breakfast this morning."

"Dad, I've been making pancakes *every* morning."

Audrey could barely deal with the pain of losing her mother. But as her father continued to speak, she realized she was losing him as well, but in a different way. They both longed for her. Yet no matter how difficult it was to face, Audrey understood that her longing would never be fulfilled. Eventually, she knew she'd have to accept the fact that her mother was gone. But her father—he could not even begin to process her death. Her life, it lingered with him. It consumed him to the point where he could not separate her body from the *life* it once possessed. Audrey feared this delusion would pull him under, like the rising river he so feared would flood the cemetery.

Her prediction a few weeks earlier had proven right; they *hadn't* make it past her mother's grave. The picnics along the river *did* stop. If only she could get him to its bank—past Mary, past the oak tree and her gravestone. There, they could sit along the river's edge and once again talk about the surfaces of other planets. She was sure it would save him. Beside the river, he would realize that *she* was still there—that *she* was an important reason to stay focused on the life they were living instead of the past he could not surrender. Getting him to the bank became her goal.

He finished the last of his sandwich and stood to touch the top of the gravestone. "Don't worry," he said. "We'll never stop being a family."

"Bye, Mom," Audrey said simply as she gathered her folding chair.

The next morning, Audrey woke with a plan. "I'm going for a walk, Dad," she said during breakfast. "Do you want to go?"

"A walk? Where to?" No longer hiding it in the cupboard, the bottle of clear liquid now sat beside his morning orange juice.

"You know, through the woods, down to the river. I want to check the water level," she lied.

"Great idea!" he shouted excitedly. He impulsively stood from the table so quickly that his chair teetered backwards and then toppled onto the stone floor. He fumbled to bring it upright. "Yes! We should go! I've been waiting all morning to tell your mother about the dream I had last night."

"But Dad—"

"You were in it, Audrey. The water, it rose up from the river. We stood by your mother's grave, trying to protect her, but it rose up the bank. It rose past our knees and over your head. We climbed onto Mary's base, but that still wasn't high enough, so we reached for her arms and pulled ourselves higher. She held us in her arms, keeping us safe from the waters. And when I turned to look at her face, it wasn't Mary at all. It was your mother—her face carved into the stone! She had saved us. We were together again, and I knew we wouldn't drown—"

"But Dad, I was just going to the river."

"Audrey, if we're going through all the trouble of tromping through the woods, then I think we can say a few words to your mother."

"I'm *not* going to see mother!" she erupted. "And if you're not going to the river with me, then don't come at all!" He grabbed his drink and finished it in one gulp. And just as he slammed the glass back to the table, she slammed the door behind her.

4
THE MEETING

She ran. She ran through the thick, muddy forest dodging vines and tree stumps, mud holes and branches. The further she ran, the more guilt she felt. Each wet leaf that struck her face was like a slap she felt should've come from her father. She questioned her devotion. How dare she deny *any* opportunity to be with her mother! She should've *wanted* to visit her grave. She should've been just as eager to tell her mother about *her* dreams! Was it possible she was letting go too easily? Was it possible she loved her mother less than he? She felt like a terrible daughter, ungrateful, uncaring.

In her frenzy, she quickly became disoriented by the weeping branches. She felt trapped and unclean. She pushed forward through the oppressive foliage until she saw a break in the trees. The sight of the clearing ahead forced her to run harder. As she recklessly neared freedom, her shoe was forced into a thick trench of mud. She toppled into the clearing, with half her body stuck in the woods and the other half in the cemetery. Although the sky was overcast, she immediately noticed how much brighter it was in the clearing compared to the dark woods. As she pulled her legs out from the trees, she watched her shoe sink beneath the mud. She lifted herself from the ground and limped a few steps inside the clearing before taking off her other shoe and throwing it to the grass.

She marched forward with every intention of heading straight to the river rushing in the distance. Yet on her way, out of the corner of her eye, there was Mary. Proving too powerful for Audrey to ignore, she soon found herself frozen in front of the statue in her stocking feet. She begged under her breath for Mary to let her pass so she could indulge in the peaceful sounds and predictable movements of the river. But there Mary stood like a symbol of her guilt, like a symbol of her mother just like in her father's dream. It was *Mary* who had protected them from the rising waters, *Mary* who had *become* her mother.

Yet Audrey was quick to separate the two. Mary was *not* her mother. Her *mother* was the one who was dead! Her *mother* was the one underground—not gloriously posing aboveground in marble! Mary was one of *them*. She held the answers to Audrey's questions. *Why was her mother taken from her? Where was she now? Could she hear her when she talked to her softly during the night?* But Mary—she wouldn't tell. She kept her secrets hidden behind her frozen face.

It took all of Audrey's strength to turn her back on the entrancing figure. She took small, careful steps through the nearest row of headstones. She tried to act casual while moving away from Mary by tapping the tops of the higher stones, as if playing a morbid game of duck-duck-goose. She traveled diagonally—until she became stuck again, this time by the crypt of Mrs. Loretta Grant.

She looked up to the gargoyles, remembering how frightened she had been of the creatures, how she would have nightmares about them breaking loose from the crypt and chasing her through the woods. But on that day, she looked into their eyes, testing them in a way, *daring* them to break free if they could. Just a few years before, she hadn't been tall enough to reach them. But that day, as she stood on her tiptoes beneath the gargoyle above the left side of the crypt's door, she was able to reach its mouth. She ran her finger over each fang. It was not sharp at all. She smiled, and then giggled to herself a bit. She was *alive*! And that meant she had power over the cemetery, power over the frozen statues and the bodies buried beneath—power over *them*. There was no need to be afraid. *She* was in control.

She thought of the apparition she had once seen. The old woman who returned from the dead to scare her when she was younger wouldn't dare show herself *now*, she reasoned. With her newfound self-assurance, she boldly cupped her hands over the crypt's window and squinted through the obscure glass. All she could see was the dead-end of a short hallway. And then suddenly something caught her eye. Near the floor, a small piece of purple fabric flowed around the corner and into the chamber! Audrey stepped back and took a deep breath. Determined not to let fear take her over, she instead laughed at her imagination—at how it had diminished the old woman into a mere fragment of what she had experienced as a child.

Next, she turned her sites up the hill. The tombstones resembled the backs of empty theater seats spread across a massive balcony. If that were so, then where she stood, between Loretta Grant's crypt and the statue of Mary, would have been center stage. A person seated near the top would've had a glorious view, as good as any bird in flight. Yet even higher, above the last row of headstones, towered Jesus.

She ran up the hill with fearless abandon. It felt good to run in her socks with mud caking beneath them. She didn't care if her feet were cold or if her white socks turned black. She felt free running carelessly over the grounds she once feared. She stopped to catch her breath near the final row of headstones. There she stood, directly beneath Jesus—yet found herself unable to look skyward. She procrastinated by turning away from him and looking down upon the cemetery. Her eyes followed the narrow gravel paths. One looped around the perimeter, and another circled Mary, the crypt, and the oak tree in the center. Yet another path led up the side of the hill to the shed, not far from where Jesus stood.

The shed was virtually hidden among the trees. It housed her father's workshop where he created all of his sculptures and carvings. And when it came to creating the statues in Ruthsford's cemetery, he spared no expense monetarily, or creatively. He didn't use cement, alabaster, sandstone, or even the typical granite. And there were no casts or molds. Each statue had been carefully carved by hand from large slabs of marble. She was amazed to think that at one time Jesus was merely an undefined block of marble, made into a figure only through the grace of her father's hands.

The shed also stored the tractor, which was powerful enough to transport her father's most bulky creations to the back of his customers' vehicles; or in the case of Mary and Jesus—to their final destinations in the cemetery. He had even custom-built a lift attached to the front of the tractor for that purpose. She imagined her father creating Jesus and then finally placing him atop the hill. What an amazing day that must've been. He must've felt triumphant!

Finally, she had gathered the nerve to turn back and look above her, quickly discovering Jesus loomed as tall as he had ever been. She would *never* grow tall enough to reach his face, or even his outstretched arms. She became dizzy looking up to him. Yet despite his indisputable stature, no longer did he seem menacing. He was only marble, merely stone fashioned by her father's hands. She had no reason to feel intimidated. She circled him, slowly at first, while running her hand over his creased robe. She then increased her pace until she found herself skipping in circles around him like he was a simple attraction on a playground. She began to sing, "Didja ever think as a hearse went by that you might be the next to die . . ." She sang in a guiltless celebration of her liberation from *them*.

And like a child on a playground, she quickly changed interests. She leapt from the top of the hill. The steep incline allowed her to travel the entire space between rows in one jump. When her feet landed, she slid even further on the moist lawn. She regained her balance and jumped again and again as she made her way down through the rows, as if playing leapfrog. Every now and then she paused to eye the river in the distance. Having conquered the cemetery, she finally felt free to play on its bank.

Yet Audrey froze where the land leveled before plummeting to the river. Once again, she found herself standing before Mary. No longer did she feel like skipping or singing. No longer was she the conqueror. Mary drained her power. Before Mary, the cemetery returned to the frightening place where the line between her and *them*, the world between the living and the unknown, was faint. It returned to the place where she could not reach the gargoyles or move her legs if frightened. So there she stayed, in front of Mary—who would not let her pass.

Audrey surrendered by sitting Indian-style on the wet ground. When she finally lifted her head, she formed a glare filled with resentment. Its intensity burned into Mary, into the figure that offered her nothing but a look of pity upon her stone face. "Did you know that her hair was naturally curly?" Audrey twirled the overgrown blades of grass between her fingers, remembering her mother's loose curls. "Or that she was a vegetarian? Or that she loved my dad? She died of cancer, you know. You probably didn't even know *that*." Her eyes began to fill. She made tight fists, but soon allowed them to go limp and fall back to the damp ground. She realized whatever force she would've mustered wouldn't have compared to the power Mary possessed. Finally, she begged for the answer she desperately needed. "Why? Why *my* mother!" But Mary would not answer.

On the outside, her expression may have been unchanging, but on the inside, Mary was crumbling. She was helpless in her constriction. She wanted to cry for Audrey. She wanted to share her emotions. She wanted to offer her comfort, wrap her arms around her. But she could do none of these things. And what pained Mary most was that she did not possess the answer Audrey begged for. For that reason only, she found herself grateful she could not speak.

Mary, however, *did* know that Audrey's mother had died from a thing called cancer, had naturally curly hair, did not eat meat, and that she loved her husband. In fact, Mary was there when Mrs. Lansly helped her husband survey the cemetery for additional plots. She was there as the two held hands, performing their nightly walk of the perimeter. She was there all the times Mrs. Lansly jogged through the cemetery and down the trails along the river. She was there when she came out to the cemetery and smoked two packs of cigarettes after her father had died. Mary was there during their family picnics along the river. She was there when, as a toddler, Audrey first visited the cemetery. And she was there when Mrs. Grant frightened little Audrey. They never knew it, but Mary was there all the while, observing, and in her own way, experiencing what it was like to be part of a family.

Audrey's resentment boiled into rage. No longer able to hold it inside, she tore off her coat and threw it to the mud. Her heart pounded, her breaths deepened. Despite the cool breeze, her face became hot. She boldly climbed upon Mary's platform. Her height only met her chin, but she had a need to confront the haunting figure. "Why!" she demanded. "Why!" She struck Mary with the side of her fist. Pain seared down her arm. She paused for a moment, letting her body absorb it, and then tightened her fist and struck her again. Soon, Audrey found herself wildly flailing her arms, unleashing her fury on the stone. With each blow, she shrieked her unanswerable question. She beat Mary until she was sure she'd be bruised. She *wanted* to be black and blue. She wanted there to be physical evidence of the pain she felt inside.

As her arms began to split open, spilling her blood on Mary's robe, the small bluebird she had seen at the house came from the woods and perched itself atop Mary's head. It cocked its head to view her actions for a moment and then dropped down, fluttering wildly beside her. Audrey stopped to look at the mysterious bird. And then, seeming satisfied just to have distracted her from her rage, it darted back into the trees, leaving just as quickly as it had come.

With the bird gone, and her rage interrupted, she stood in silence, alone, and was once again overcome with her familiar childhood feelings. The cemetery had closed in on her. Jesus loomed forward, watching her from the sky like a disapproving giant. She could feel the evil stare of the gargoyles hanging from the crypt. And she sensed the spirit of Loretta Grant creeping slowly behind her: her dead, pale hands covered in tawdry rings, reaching for the back of her neck. She quickly spun around fully expecting to see the dead woman, but did not.

Suddenly feeling the full impact of her outburst, she whimpered in short breaths of agony. She examined the damage done to Mary. Nothing. Only *her* blood was on the front of the statue. It was useless. Her rage proved insignificant. She let her arms hang, dripping beside her. The battle had ended. She had been defeated. And only once she admitted this to herself, did the cemetery seem to grant her normality again.

The openness returned. Clouds gave way to sunlight. The air swept the ground beside her and swirled up to her face, cooling her heated skin. Her hair began to dry in the light wind. And in the oak tree above, a leaf had been holding a drop of rainwater in its crease. The warm rays of sun, coupled with the delicate breeze, caused the leaf to unravel, finally letting go of the water. On its descent, the drip was able to avoid all of the other leaves and branches; it landed in the corner of Mary's eye. Audrey lifted her head just as the tear ran down Mary's face. She staggered back a step, amazed by the site. The morning sun hung behind Mary. It seemed the first time that summer the sun had shown; its light formed a blazing halo around Mary's head.

Audrey was stunned. "I—I'm so sorry! I didn't know!" she cried. She squinted at the illuminated Mary, who *did* cry and who *did* bleed! It was—a miracle! "I'm so sorry," she repeated, ashamed. But she knew her words weren't enough. The site of her blood on Mary sickened her. Her sacrilege was not something she could simply apologize for, so she ceased her attempt. Instead, she hung her head and began to speak in a soft, hushed tone—a far cry from the defiant voice she had used only moments before. "My dad—he's always afraid the wrong people might find this place," she whispered, shuffling her feet, hoping to appease Mary. "You know, trash it or something."

Mary knew.

She heard movement in the woods. Branches rustling, twigs snapping. She quickly jumped from the platform and grabbed her coat from the wet ground. She used it to frantically wipe the blood from Mary's robe. When she heard the movement approach the clearing, she hung onto Mary's waist and twisted behind her, dropping herself out of site. There, hidden behind Mary, she watched as he emerged from the trees. She worried he would see her shoe abandoned at the edge of the cemetery, but he made a straight line for his wife's grave, his fists tucked firmly in the pockets of his flannel coat. Audrey wrapped her own coat around her arms to slow the bleeding.

He knelt before Mary, not caring if his knees got wet. "Good morning, honey." He looked to the sky. "I'm glad to see the sun's out. You certainly deserve it." His hand caressed the ground. "Have you seen Audrey? She's out here somewhere." He paused, recalling their argument. "Ah, of course. She's gone to the river." He scanned the riverbank for a moment before returning his deep stare to the young grass he knelt upon. "I know what she must think—that there's no reason for us to visit you here—that we don't have to be here for you to hear us. But to me, when we're here, when we're close to you, it feels like we're a family again. I don't know," he lowered his head. "Maybe she's right."

He felt at that moment the overwhelming need to be closer to her. He scooped up a section of wet sod, exposing its roots. He set it aside and watched worms move freely in the soft soil. Water quickly filled the crevices, forming tiny pools. He pulled up another section, and soon the unstable soil surrounding the hole he had created caved in, filling it once more. Frustrated, he scooped out the mud and threw it with all his might. It hit a nearby headstone, splattering across the name and date. Yet by the time he looked to the hole again, fresh dirt had already crumbled in its place. It was no use. He stood up, defeated. "Maybe she's right," he whispered.

Audrey heard him walk away and peered from behind Mary. To her surprise, he did not head back through the woods, but instead walked towards the river. He stood at the bank. "Audrey!" he called out, once downriver and once upriver. She wanted to run to him and apologize, but remained shielded behind Mary massaging her aching arms.

He waited a moment for her response and then unbuttoned his work shirt. With his jeans still on, he dove into the glistening river. He reappeared in its center, his head just a blur amid the bright sun reflecting off the water. Audrey watched as he washed the mud from his hands and arms and then crawled back onto the bank. There he lay on his back, soaking up the sun like a cat let outside for the first time in the summer.

Slowly and quietly, Audrey stood from behind Mary and hopped back upon her platform. She kissed her hardened hand. "Thank you," she whispered. Her father had made it to the river. And as he sunbathed on its bank, Audrey grabbed her shoes and crept back through the trees.

5
THE FIRE

Mary knew what was going to happen that night. She could tell by the position of the setting sun, by the hot mist that hovered between the trees, and by the specific tint of color on the leaves. But most of all, she knew what was about to happen when she saw Mr. Lansly and Audrey unfold the tattered red blanket. They placed it just past the last row of headstones before the river. Each year on this same day, the Lanslys would sit on the blanket and watch fire from hell spurt from the earth and into the sky. After Mrs. Lansly's death, Mary thought she'd never see the old blanket again, but there it was. She was happy to see it.

The fire was glorious. Each year, it rose above the tree line, shooting to the sky in slim streaks of multi-colored light. Then, just when the trails of light looked as if they would touch the horizon, they would burst into hundreds of colorful sparks. The sparks would reflect onto the river as they twinkled back to the earth. These eruptions repeated over and over, several at a time. The fire would light up the dark sky. It would fill the night with the sound of loud explosions—until suddenly, the dazzling display would cease and leave the evening silent once again.

Despite its beauty, the fire terrified Mary. It scared her *because* it was so beautiful. She wondered how something that came from such a horrible place, a place of eternal torture and fire, could create something so spectacular. She felt guilt for anticipating it, for wishing she could see it every night instead of just once a year. These feelings confused her. Should she not have allowed herself to indulge in its wonder?

Audrey pulled a thin wire out from a box and held it towards her dad, who in turn held out his lighter. Mary watched as his small flame met with the tip of the wire. Immediately, tiny sparks erupted—like a smaller version of the fire in the sky. It reminded Mary of the orange flowers that lined the edge of the woods in the spring. Yet, unlike those flowers, Audrey's orange flower had a sparkling blossom, spraying its flickers of fire down the stem she held. Audrey held a sparkling flower in each hand and made like an airplane, weaving between headstones with her arms outstretched. Twice she circled Mary before hopping onto her platform. There, she carefully bent one of the wires and slid it between Mary's fingers. "Happy Fourth of July, Mary," she said before flying back to the blanket.

Mary looked down to the flower of light, not feeling the sparks hit her hand. "It's so beautiful! Can you all see it?" Mary asked the others. Bluebell flew to a low branch of the oak to get a closer view. Impressed, he chirped a happy tune.

Jesus, however, quickly squelched her indulgence. "You're holding hellfire in your hand, correct?" He questioned her like a pompous professor who already knew the answer, but pushed his pupil to think for herself. "It's evil, Mary. You should fear it."

"But it's just—so beautiful. I don't understand. How can something this beautiful be evil? Are *flowers* evil?"

"Satan is devious and can mislead. Isn't that what Bluebell told us? So if you believe your Strange Man, the fire—it may be the most beautiful thing you've ever seen, but that doesn't make it any less evil."

"But the Lanslys—they watch the fire every year! They enjoy it. And Audrey, she gave this to me to enjoy. Certainly *she's* not evil." Jesus refused to answer, letting his silence stun Mary's thoughts.

"Maybe they don't know about evil," offered Bluebell. "I've rarely seen them at the church, Mary."

"Mrs. Grant never went to church either!" shouted Gareth.

"And look where it got her," Jesus promptly added, "trapped in the cemetery with us."

"You don't mean to say that someone is evil just because they don't listen to the Strange Man?"

"You don't see anyone else who's buried floating around here, do you?"

"No. But maybe all the others are just lying there—like nothing. Like there was nothing before them and nothing afterwards. Gone. Erased." She watched as the sparkles on the wire came to the end. Light smoke replaced the orange flickers until it was just a wire again. "Maybe Mrs. Grant is the lucky one," she suggested.

"Well, why don't you ask her? Maybe she can tell you if she's damned or if she's blessed."

"Yeah! Wake up Mrs. Whitehead!" hollered Arthur.

Gareth was eager to volunteer. "Let me do it. I'll rustle the old bones!"

"Don't you remember?" asked Mary. "She *never* comes out when the fires erupt. It marks the day she was married."

"What a day to get married," Jesus remarked.

"Last year, she cried all night. How sad."

"Boo hoo hoo in her purple tissue!" shouted Gareth.

"Boo hoo hoo!" Arthur joined in. Soon, both gargoyles gleefully repeated their exaggerated impersonation of Mrs. Grant—until finally, across the river, a small flicker of light rose into the sky.

"Mary, I think it's starting," Bluebell whispered in her ear.

Mary enjoyed the colorful eruptions, but also admired the father and daughter who sat on the blanket beneath them. She had always been thankful for her caretaker and his family. So to her, the notion that Audrey or her father may be evil—or that they may be blind to evil—was incomprehensible.

In the recent weeks, Mary had grown particularly fond of Audrey. After their first meeting under the morning sun, Audrey visited her every day. On some days, she would trace the grooves in Mary's hands while singing hushed ditties so silent, Mary couldn't make them out. Yet on most days, she would simply stare up to Mary for hours.

Audrey stared, thinking that if she watched her long enough, perhaps Mary would move, perhaps she would speak. Sometimes she would stare at her until the sun sank to the river and turned pink, until her father came to walk her back to the house. He didn't mind her unusual hobby. In fact, he was overjoyed she was spending so much time in the cemetery—although he had no idea that it was Mary, not his wife, who held her focus for all those hours.

In a way, Mary's wish had come true. She loved having a child visit her. And finally, unlike the mourners, she had a visitor who had gotten past the dreadful stage of asking *why?* Still, Mary wished there was some way she could communicate with Audrey. She wanted to let her know that she was in fact aware of her presence. She wanted to have conversations with her. She wanted to offer her comfort, peace.

And on that night under the fiery sky, Mary felt something else—something more powerful than her natural affinity for the Lanslys; she wished she could've filled the empty spot on the blanket. She wanted to be *with them*, pointing as they pointed to their favorite colored explosions. She wanted to feel the warm wind. She wanted to shield Audrey with her robe should any sparks land too close. She agonized over the distance to the river as would a mother unable to be with her child.

Soon after the last of the bright sparkles disappeared from the sky, Mr. Lansly and Audrey folded their blanket. He placed his arm around her, and she carried the flashlight as they found their way back through the trees.

"More glorious than last year!" announced Mary. Bluebell whistled, delightfully agreeing. "Wouldn't you say so, Gareth?"

"I've seen better."

"When? The last two years you've shut your eyes because you were so frightened of the noise! You liked it, didn't you, Arthur?"

"Oh my! I don't know where to start. It was the most amazing spectacle I've ever seen! Why the colors alone are sure to blind me for days!" he gushed.

"See. I knew Bluebell and I weren't the only ones who enjoyed the fire," Mary said, not alerted to his sarcasm. "What about you, Jesus?"

"I'm not letting my eyes deceive me. You must stop thinking that everything beautiful is pure."

"But the fire *is* pure," she said boldly. "In fact, I'd love to see that lake of fire up close. I'll bet it's the most magnificent sight to see!" Declaring aloud what she thought to be true made her feel liberated. It made her feel as if there was *something* about the world around her she could be certain she believed.

But Jesus gasped. "You shouldn't even joke about that, Mary. It's deceit. You let Satan fool you too easily."

And as quickly as it had come, Jesus had taken away her self-assurance, transforming it into guilt and worry. What if he was right? What if she was in fact being tricked into loving things that were evil? Bluebell had said that "Sin is when you do something wrongful in the eyes of God." She wondered if finding beauty in something created by Satan was wrongful in the eyes of God. She wondered if she was a sinner.

But then, Mary cleared her head and thought for a moment. It thrilled her to see the colored lights in the evening. And she was *glad* Mrs. Grant wasn't like the rest of them, rotting away. And she adored Audrey. So if it was true that Satan was responsible for the fire, for its beauty. If perhaps he was responsible for Mrs. Grant's ability to stay earthbound. If he had any influence over Audrey's kindness, her sense of wonder—then Mary couldn't force herself to see him as evil. And she couldn't see how she could've sinned.

Mary knew the people at the church spoke of *worshipping* the "heavenly father," meaning God. But she didn't personally know the heavenly father. Or Satan for that matter. Even if she *was* created by God, it didn't seem right to worship someone whom she never met. So at that moment, she made a decision. She would simply worship life itself. She would worship beauty. She would worship the fire, the flowers, the trees, wind, and grass. She would worship the sky, Mrs. Grant, Mr. Lansly, and Audrey. She could see them. They mattered to her.

6
THE PARTY

Bluebell cocked his head. "Someone's coming," he chirped.

Mary scanned the bank. "Have they left something behind?"

Two beams of light flickered in the darkness between the trees. The lights bobbed back and forth and then crisscrossed. They appeared to move aimlessly at first, floating towards and then away from the cemetery, but soon their intended destination was clear.

"Is it Mr. Lansly?" wondered Gareth.

"Is he coming back to check on us?" asked Arthur

"No," said Bluebell. "Someone's coming from the *road*."

Above their whispers and the chirping crickets, a young woman's long-winded laugh filled the forest. Immediately, Mary became excited. Would she be blessed with more life around her, more beauty to worship? She relished the rare sound of laughter and could not wait to meet the person on the other end of the happy, careless tones.

"Shit! My shoe's stuck in the mud!" Julie shrieked.

"Just take it off. Here, I'll carry you," said Greg, followed by more high-pitched giggles from Julie.

"Greg, what's down this old two-track anyway?" asked Marlene, another young woman, sounding cautious yet curious.

"This!" he declared. The pair of beams slowly scanned the cemetery from atop the hill. Mary watched as one of the beams passed above her shoulder, creating moving shadows out of the tombstones and blades of grass.

Immediately, the giggling stopped. "You took us to a *cemetery?* You're an idiot," declared Julie.

"Calm down. Let's at least get a closer look."

"It's awesome, huh?" said Jack, who gripped the other flashlight. Together, the two couples made their way down the hill in a huddled group. "Greg and I found this place when we were hiking last year."

Mary remembered. It was a late summer evening when the two young men appeared from the trail along the river. She even remembered the color of their backpacks: one blue, the other red. They poked around the cemetery a bit, and like many of the young, were fascinated by Mrs. Grant's crypt. After realizing they could not see into its main chamber, the young men stripped and jumped in the river to cool off. Their splashing and hollering must've carried to the house because Mr. Lansly rushed through the woods with his shotgun. "Get the hell out of here! This is no swimming hole!" he bellowed. The pair was barely able to gather their clothes before scattering back down the trail.

Marlene grabbed the flashlight from Jack and boldly ran to the center of the cemetery, bringing herself into Mary's view. As she spun in wonderment, Mary admired her dark, flowing hair. "This is it!" she declared. "I've heard about this place, but never knew it really existed." Jack joined her under the oak tree. He was as Mary had remembered him, except for the thin beard he had grown.

"There are myths about the Ruthsford cemetery," Marlene continued. "Stories of people hiking here and never being seen again. People claiming to see ghosts move between the headstones. And some say that if you stand real still on a day when the wind is low, you can hear voices. Some think they are the voices of spirits, while others say the voices actually come from the statues themselves—that if you listen real close, you can hear their secret conversations." She slowly moved the beam of her flashlight up Mary's robe and held it on her face.

Mary squinted into the bright light. When Marlene finally lowered the light, she saw Greg approaching, with Julie not far behind. Julie clutched the back of Greg's tee-shirt, limping forward with only one shoe. Mary couldn't take her eyes off her. Her hair! She had never seen anything like it. It was so blonde, and so tall. She wondered how she got it to stand atop her head so high. And her face! Her eyelids were painted blue, and her cheeks painted red. Mary loved how colorful she was.

"I don't get why people don't know about this place," said Greg.

Marlene chuckled as she aimed her flashlight at his shoes, which were covered in thick mud. "Maybe it has something to do with how hard it is to get here."

Eager to explore, Marlene quickly moved down a row of headstones. "Look at how old some of these are!" She bent over, shining her flashlight at the barely legible weathered inscriptions for a closer look. "This person died in 1873." She traced the faded 8 with her finger. Jack startled her by gently placing his hand on her hip. She spun around, and the flashlight became pressed between the two of them, making them appear to glow from their abdomens.

"So I guess you're not mad we brought you here then?" he asked, wrapping his arms around her.

"I think it's beautiful," she gushed. "I love it!"

"Well I think it's gross!" Julie fumed. She stood with her arms folded, glaring at Greg. "What kind of sickos would take their girlfriends to a *cemetery?*"

"At least take a look around," suggested Marlene. "You have to see these carvings."

"I'd rather not."

"I know what will get that laughter back in your voice," said Greg. He grabbed Julie's shoulders and guided her closer to Jack and Marlene. He then lightly pushed her in their direction as if letting go of a child learning how to ride a bike. "The beer. I set it down in the woods when I picked you up. Be right back."

With no interest in the monuments, Julie grudgingly sat beneath the oak tree, leaving Jack and Marlene to explore by themselves.

"Where do they come from?" asked Jesus.

"I don't know," said Bluebell. He hopped down to a lower branch of the oak for a closer look.

"Do they go to the church?" he asked.

"Oh Jesus, what does it matter?" Mary sighed.

"No," answered Bluebell. "They're not from the town."

"What was that noise!" Julie shouted to Jack and Marlene as she nervously looked to the above branches.

"It's probably just a bird or some squirrel that lives in the tree," Jack assured her. "Relax. They're dead. They can't hurt you."

Jack hung back while Marlene stepped up to the door of the crypt. She examined the gargoyles for a moment before reaching for Arthur's face. "Get this girl out of my nose!" he squealed as Mary laughed. And as if Marlene had heard him, she abruptly pulled her hand away. Out of the corner of her eye, something else had caught her attention—a flicker of movement beside the crypt. Bravely, she took a step towards the corner of the tomb. She held onto her flashlight firmly as she rounded the corner, but there was nothing there. She pressed forward to investigate if anything was stirring behind the crypt. And before she knew it, without warning, a dark figure lunged towards her! She jumped backwards, dropping the flashlight.

"Gotcha!" shouted Greg.

But it was Julie several yards away, not Marlene, who screamed. The high-pitched shriek rung throughout the forest until all the breath in her lungs had been exhausted. "You bastard!" she cried when she realized what had happened.

"Real funny, Greg," added Marlene as she bent down to retrieve the flashlight.

Greg strutted out from behind the crypt with the case of beer curled under his arm like a football. A duffel bag was slung over his shoulder. The four regrouped beneath the oak. "Now no more screaming," he ordered as he threw the bag to Jack. He opened the case of beer and took one for himself. "There's a psycho guy who lives around here, the caretaker I guess. He tried to chase us off before."

"Well I wouldn't have screamed if you weren't such an ass!" Julie shouted, and then yanked a beer from the case.

"You know the crypt you were looking at, Marlene?" asked Greg. "Well, I heard the lady who's in there hacked up her husband because she found out he had a mistress."

"Another one of your bullshit stories," claimed Jack.

"No. I actually think he's right," said Marlene. "I remember my friend Anne telling me something about it. Her grandmother used to live in Ruthsford."

"She waited 'til he went to bed," Greg continued, "and then, with a butcher's knife taken from the very restaurant they owned, she carved out his insides."

"That's not true! She didn't kill him!" Mary pleaded to closed ears. Yet even with her assuredness, she, the gargoyles, Jesus and Bluebell listened intently to the rest of Greg's story.

"And after she took care of him, she ran to the basement of their mansion and tied one end of a rope to a pipe in the ceiling, and made a noose around her neck with the other end." He grabbed his throat and stuck out his tongue. "She hung herself while her husband's guts still oozed across their bedroom floor."

"Gross!" cried Julie, hugging herself.

"And tonight—" his eyes widened, "Tonight is the anniversary. His murder, her suicide; it happened on the Fourth of July."

"No! It's their *wedding* anniversary!" Mary protested.

"I knew it!" Jesus shouted. "I knew there had to be a good reason she's stuck in this cemetery!"

"Don't be ridiculous!" said Mary. "He made that story up. I'm sure of it!"

"Well tomorrow when she comes out, let's ask her."

"*Ask her! Ask her!*" the gargoyles challenged.

"We can't! We can't ask her *that*," said Mary. "It would be—rude!"

Despite her defense of Mrs. Grant, Mary secretly wondered if she was a murderer, if Mrs. Grant was in fact evil. As she watched the teens drown themselves in alcohol, she wondered if Jesus *had* been right. *Was* the cemetery Mrs.

Grant's punishment? It certainly would answer why she was the sole apparition. It seemed just when she was sure of something, Mary was forced to question herself all over again.

The teens drank until Julie once again let out a string of giggles, until Greg stood up and took off his shirt. "The river's just over there," he pointed. "I'm going for a swim." He finished undressing on his way to the bank.

Julie swayed as she followed him. "Wait for me!" she called ahead, attempting to run, undress, and giggle at the same time. Soon they were all in the water. "Eeww! There's mud between my toes," Julie complained while laughing. She then waved her arms upon the water's surface, splashing uncontrollably.

"You know, that guy had a gun with him," Greg warned her.

"I can't help it!" she screeched. "I love the water!"

"That guy—what do you plan to do if he comes back again?" Marlene asked Jack.

Before Jack could answer, Greg punched him lightly in the shoulder and motioned to the duffel bag still near the oak tree. "I think it's time for a little payback," he said. He crawled out of the river and snatched the bag. When he returned to the bank, he held it high over his head as he dripped. "Behold—paybacks!" He lowered the bag to his chest and unzipped it. Jack climbed out of the water to join him.

"What are you going to do?" asked Marlene.

"The party's just beginning," announced Greg as he unpacked his arsenal of toilet paper rolls, cans of spray paint and two cartons of eggs. "You really want to see some fireworks?" He ran to the oak tree with a roll of toilet paper. He hung onto the end and flung the rest of the roll as high as he could. It wrapped around a branch near the top of the tree before falling back to the ground like a giant streamer. Again and again, he tossed the roll. Towards the end of the roll, he no longer cared about the precision of his throws. He threw it blindly over his head, even tossing it from between his legs.

Enthralled by his antics, Julie brought herself out of the water. She lay with her stomach on the bank for a moment, too happy with snickers to immediately stand. When she finally found the strength to lift herself upright, she too grabbed a roll of toilet paper and ran to Greg. Tugging on his arm, she led him to Mary's platform. She stood behind Mary while Greg stood in front. Giggling, she placed the end of the tissue under her foot and unrolled it to arm's length. She then tossed it to Greg on the other side, and they began circling Mary from the bottom up.

"Look how beautiful, Bluebell! They're decorating me," Mary gushed.

Bluebell, cowering deep within the tree, said "I don't think it's decoration, Mary."

"It's *desecration!*" roared Jesus.

Jack grabbed a can of spray paint and headed up the hill. "Stop it!" shouted Marlene, finally climbing out of the river. She grabbed the toilet paper from Greg's hands and tossed it to the ground. "You can't ruin this place!"

Undeterred, Greg strolled over to the eggs. He picked up an egg, rolling it lightly in his hand while nodding up the hill to Jack. "Why don't you worry about your own boyfriend?" Having said that, he pitched the egg perfectly into Gareth's face. The shell burst, and the clear and yellow ooze slid down his face and dripped from his fangs.

Marlene ran to the base of the hill. She could barely make out Jack's figure in the darkness, but she could hear the clanking of the metal mixing ball each time he shook the can. "Jack, get the hell down here!"

"He chased us off with a gun!" he yelled down to her. "He could've killed us!"

"You're just drunk. Let's go!" When it became clear none of them would listen to reason, she alone marched back up the muddy path and through the darkened woods. "I can't believe this!" she fumed as she headed for the car.

Greg held the carton as he threw eggs at headstones, pretending he was shooting targets. He'd choose certain markers and then assess the accuracy of his hits. When he ran out of eggs, he grabbed a rock and shattered Mrs. Grant's small window. Jack came down from the hill and began spray-painting the portions of Mary that shown from beneath the toilet paper. Julie bounced up and down, throwing rolls of toilet paper over her head in no apparent direction. Some flew up into the tree, while others bounced off Mary's arms and head.

His friends could not move, much less protect themselves, so Bluebell did what he could. He tried to deter the intruders by flapping over their heads. He dove again and again, narrowly escaping the streams of toilet paper that randomly sprung into the air. But he was a small bird, and his movements went unnoticed. He knew he alone could not defend them. And without the Lanslys, he knew there was only one other who could.

High in the oak tree, a branch creaked loudly as it bent almost to its breaking point. Julie froze with a roll of toilet paper in her hand and gazed uneasily to the tree above. It was disorienting, looking up into the multitude of white streams gently swaying in the midnight breeze. "Get over here!" she whispered urgently, motioning to Greg and Jack. The three of them peered up into the tree as Julie pointed to where she had heard the noise.

Then, as if from out of a dream, she came. Black high-heeled shoes slowly found their way between the high branches. And as the shoes came closer, it was apparent they were connected to legs. And as the legs came into view, it became obvious they belonged to the body of a woman. Dangling from the rope tied tightly around her neck, Mrs. Grant slowly descended from the branches. She came into full view amid the flowing toilet paper, making it appear as if she were floating underwater. Her purple dress never looked so tattered. Her face was never as pale, her hair never as white. She was absolutely beautiful. Her body bobbed and swayed with every movement of the rickety branch as the rope lowered her into frightening recognition.

Julie's mouth wasn't large enough for the shriek that her lungs produced. Greg and Jack ran in disarray, stumbling over headstones hidden by the cascading web of toilet paper. Chaos swirled around them in flashes of purple and white. In the excitement, Bluebell flew into a strip of flowing paper. He became tangled in the light fabric and tumbled out of control. Greg, seeing the strip of paper flutter towards him, batted it with his arm.

Through her eye that wasn't covered by toilet paper, Mary watched the teens finally retreat from the cemetery, once again leaving nearly all their clothes behind. She then peered to the ground before her and was sickened to see a light-blue feather gently saunter to the white-covered earth. The next morning, Bluebell was not to be found.

7
MRS. GRANT

Broken tissue blew across Audrey's shoes as she stood in disbelief. Overnight, the cemetery had been transformed. It looked as if a tacky circus show had been operating on the site and then left abruptly before dawn. Toilet paper covered the ground. It fluttered gently in the breeze like drifting snow. It hung from the branches of the oak, transforming the space beneath it into what looked to Audrey like a colossal, yet tattered tepee.

As she cautiously moved forward, she noticed cracked eggs had dried on the faces of several tombstones, while other tombstones were marked with streaks of paint. Profanities covered the walls of the crypt. And worst of all, the statues had been transformed into disgraced versions of their former selves. The gargoyles were reduced to looking like cartoon characters, now in vibrant shades of blue, red and yellow. Jesus' robe looked as if a child had wildly took giant crayons to him. And Mary—she too appeared to have been painted, at least between the loose gaps in the reams of toilet paper, which wrapped her like a mummy from her base to her head.

At once, uncontrollable feelings of guilt and shame flooded Audrey. She quickly stepped past Mary, hoping she would not be seen. She scurried towards where the toilet paper parted beneath the oak, the entrance of the "tepee," and slipped inside. There, beneath the tree, behind the thin strands, she hid from the statues—embarrassed, mortified. How could this have happened as she and her father slept just on the other side of the trees? A dizzying sense of hopelessness filled her as she rubbed her arms, unsure of what to do.

"Where were you!" a voice rasped from above. Audrey looked above her to see the pointed heel of a woman's black shoe just inches from her face. She jolted back a step. Tattered purple fabric fluttered alongside the tattered toilet paper. "The least you could do is give us an answer." The old woman looked peculiar. She sat on the lowest branch of the tree like only a young child would, her legs dangling.

As soon as Audrey made eye contact with her, her lips formed a pout. And then like a spoiled child disapproving of Audrey's mere presence, she promptly grabbed hold of her dress, re-crossed her legs and turned her head the other way. Seeming unable to sit still for very long, she then began fidgeting with the thick rope tied around her neck, which descended from high within the tree.

Audrey knew who she was. Mrs. Grant needed no introduction. "You *are* real!" She stepped towards her, more amazed than afraid. She was there physically, solid. Audrey had the urge to touch the fabric of her dress. She wanted to know what she felt like. But before she could get close enough, Mrs. Grant resumed her icy glare upon Audrey.

"We're not here to talk about me, young lady. I know all there is to know about that. Believe me, I've had a few years to think about it."

"There's a rope around your neck," Audrey said spontaneously, not intending the words to pass her lips.

"My. An observant child. No doubt you have the mysteries of the universe figured out." She slipped the noose over her head.

Audrey couldn't take her eyes off Mrs. Grant. It was her imagination sitting right in front of her, alive and speaking. Only it *wasn't* her imagination! As Audrey had gotten older, part of her began to wonder if her view of the cemetery had been mistakenly built upon childish fantasies, daydreams and nightmares. But that curious, frightened child who had seen Mrs. Grant for the first time remained inside her. And seeing the old woman again, having a conversation with her, was that child's vindication. It confirmed there was reality behind what she had come near to dismissing as imagination and personal myth.

Mrs. Grant tugged on the bulky rope. It let loose and came spiraling through the branches directly above Audrey. Audrey hunched over and covered her head, but the rope dissolved into the air. Instead of jumping down and collapsing to the ground as one might expect an old woman sitting on a branch would, Mrs. Grant simply slid down the bowing branch as if it were a playground slide. Audrey braced for her high heels to dig into the dirt upon her dismount, but Mrs. Grant's shoes never touched the ground. She simply hovered several inches above the earth. Gravity had no effect on her. "Whatever happened to your father being so protective?" Mrs. Grant heightened her pitch to mimic Audrey's voice. "'My dad's always afraid the wrong people might find this place. You know, trash it or something.'"

"You were listening?" asked Audrey, beginning to feel intimidated.

"And what have I got better to do, young lady? Now tell me. Where was he? Where was he with that flashlight of his?"

"It was after the fireworks. He was—in bed. It was late!" Audrey took a deep breath and reminded herself she was shouting at a ghost.

"And where were *you?*"

"I was in bed too."

Mrs. Grant cupped her hand under her chin. She turned away from Audrey and took several steps. "What about Mary?" she whispered.

"What?" Audrey didn't understand.

Mrs. Grant twisted to face Audrey again. Her dress twirled around her, trying to keep up with her rapid movements. "I said, try telling that to Mary!" she croaked. Her bony finger permeated the thinness of the blowing toilet paper and pointed towards the mummified Mary.

Audrey poked her head out of the tepee. "You mean she's real too? She can hear me!"

"Of course she can, dear." Mrs. Grant twisted her wrist, and a thin cigarette appeared between her fingers. She took a long drag and exhaled toward the opening at the top of the tree. "And let me tell you, she's lucky that's all those degenerates did to her. A busted arm is nothing to take by chance."

Audrey tore out from under the tree. Mrs. Grant hovered behind her as she ran for Mary. Audrey jumped upon her platform. The charred wire poked out from beneath the layers of toilet paper. She plucked out the dead sparkler and threw it to the ground. "I knew it!" she shouted as she began to furiously uncover her, ripping through the paper and tossing it aside. She frantically rubbed Mary's hand like a genie's lamp. "Talk to me," Audrey pleaded. "It's okay! I know you can talk to me now!"

"She can't *talk* to you." Mrs. Grant sat with her legs folded at the edge of the platform. "You better just settle down, missy."

"You said she can hear me. She *must* be able to talk! *You* can talk. I can hear *you!*"

"She's a statue, dear. Statues lips aren't made for speaking, but their ears are made for listening. Their eyes are made for seeing."

"So *all* the statues can hear me? They can *see* me?" Audrey eyed the bizarre gargoyles, whose power of fright had been diminished to a mockery. She looked to Jesus. The vandals could not reach above his arms, but had effectively ruined the lower part of his robe. "I'm sorry to you all!" she cried. She leaned her back against Mary and closed her eyes. "I'm sorry to you all," she repeated in a weak voice.

Mrs. Grant cleared her throat, and Audrey's eyes sprung open. "So? What are you going to do?" she barked, towering over her.

"Oh no! You're right! I have to fix it!" Audrey thought not only of the statues, but also of her father. She knew if he saw the cemetery in that condition, he would be devastated. "My dad—he went into town, but he'll be back anytime now. He can't see it like this!"

She worked quickly to finish removing the toilet paper from Mary, and then attempted to demolish the tepee by circling the tree and yanking down the fluttering strips. As she accumulated armfuls, she added the tissue to a pile she had started in front of Mary's platform. Yet after what seemed like endless trips to and from the oak tree, little more than a dent had been made in the work that needed to be done. "It's no use," she complained as she surveyed her work. There was less toilet paper on the lower part of the tree, but it was now cut off in unreachable, jagged strips.

Audrey sat overwhelmed amid the pile of soft tissue. She wanted to give up, wanted to stay there forever. She lay on her back and reached her arms out as far as she could over her head—and then realized she was stretched beside her mother's grave. Though she appeared solid, Mrs. Grant easily passed through the marker and stood over Audrey as a not-so-subtle reminder of the task she had yet to complete. Yet despite Mrs. Grant's powerful persuasion, Audrey instead concentrated on the lettering she had so effortlessly traveled through.

The inscription only contained basic information, only numbers and words: *Beloved Wife and Mother,*" it read. Audrey had never felt a gravestone was an adequate representation of her mother, or of anyone else for that matter. But since confirming Mrs. Grant's existence, she thought perhaps it didn't need to be. Mrs. Grant was what her mother had become—someone who lingered on the other side of reality: behind mirrors, in dreams, as an apparition in a graveyard. However unfathomable, Audrey now knew it was true; her mother was one of *them.* Yet she was certain the sight of the old woman meant that she would see her mother again. Furthermore, it convinced her she wouldn't have to die to be with her either.

Audrey decided she was prepared to see the new form her mother had taken. "Where's my mother?" she asked, looking up to Mrs. Grant. "When do I get to see her?"

"See her? I assume you have a picture."

"No. See her like I see you. Like—a ghost."

Mrs. Grant began to cackle. She cackled until her old face began to sag, until it took on a most serious tone. "*I'm* the only ghost in this cemetery. I can assure you."

Audrey sat upright to face Mrs. Grant. "But she's dead. You're dead!"

"Do you think all it takes for one to become a ghost is to be deceased? If it was that easy, the cemeteries of the world would be overcrowded. This way, I have the run of the place. And in my opinion, it's only fair."

"But what about the rest of them?" Audrey looked to the hundreds of headstones. "What about my mom?"

"I'm not God." She levitated to Mary's platform. "If I were, I wouldn't be stuck here, now would I? I did not ask for this spot." Mrs. Grant pointed to her mother's grave. "And she did not ask for hers, but that's where she is." She threw her cigarette to the ground. It burst into a tiny flame before Audrey's feet and then disappeared. "You're asking the wrong person."

"That's it then? She's just—in the ground!"

"Young lady, I'm not a Bible. The only thing golden about me is this damn ring, and it's given me nothing but a skin rash!"

Audrey was silent. *Was death useless? Did it serve no purpose?* She never thought of it as something to look forward to, but she had hoped when someone died, they at least ended up in a better place. Yet according to Mrs. Grant, even *her* miserable condition was like winning the lottery. Audrey scanned the cemetery. She felt its emptiness. The stones only marked the absence of what once was.

"I hate to ruin your meditating, dear, but you *do* have more than an ample amount of work to finish."

Ironically, it took Mrs. Grant to snap her back to reality. Audrey stood from the matted paper and noticed the blue streaks of paint on Mary. "I'll try to get that off," she said mechanically. "There must be some kind of cleaner in the shed." Audrey began to trudge her way up the hill.

"Stop!" ordered Mrs. Grant before she got too far. Audrey froze. "For some unknown reason to which I'm sure I'll never know the answer, Mary has said that she *likes* the blue on her. In fact, blue happens to be her favorite color."

"*You* can hear her? Why didn't you tell me!"

"Well of course I can hear her. I'm dead. I can hear a lot of things you can't."

Audrey quickly scanned the ground until she found the blue can of spray paint sticking out from under a layer of toilet paper. "How would Mary like an *entire robe* of blue?" She shook the can.

Mrs. Grant rolled her eyes. "This is quite unnecessary, don't you think?"

"What did she say?" Audrey persisted.

Mrs. Grant let out a sigh as she sat back down on Mary's platform, her dress surrounding her in a pool of purple. "She said it would be beautiful," she repeated with far less enthusiasm than Mary had intended.

Audrey was happy to comply. She began by carefully applying the paint in the folded creases of her robe. She took her time, knowing Mary's clothes were permanent. "I think you're very pretty," she told her. "I would've painted you a blue robe a long time ago if I would've known." Mrs. Grant yawned with disinterest as she adjusted her dress. "I *knew* you were alive," Audrey continued. "I could tell all along that you were my friend. I used to have a lot of friends, but I don't have any this summer. I had a good friend named Donna. She called once, but my dad says it's too long of a drive to pick her up, or drop me off—even though he did it last summer." She stopped spraying for a moment. "But I guess he has a lot to do. Anyway, I don't mind. Not anymore."

"I have a good friend," Mary said through Mrs. Grant. "Only I don't know where he is. I'm so worried about him, Audrey. Something happened to him last night."

"I'm sorry. What does he look like? Maybe I could help you find him."

"Oh, you would be able to hear him singing. I keep listening for him. He has the most beautiful blue feathers and a brown chest. He lives in an old fence along the road."

"A bird? A bluebird? In Michigan?" Audrey knew which bird Mary spoke of.

"Yes. His name is Bluebell."

Even though her words came through in Mrs. Grant's voice, Audrey could sense her worry and anxiety. She remembered the tiny bird watching her through the windows and made a realization. She gazed up to Mary's smooth face. "Then you were there too," she said, realizing that as he had watched over her, so too did Mary. Understanding just how important he was to her, Audrey couldn't help but feel guilt over his disappearance. "I'll check the path as soon as I'm done here," she promised.

"Oh thank you, Audrey. I would appreciate that!"

Slowly, Mrs. Grant faded. Despite even her uninspired translation, she slipped into the background. She became the mediator, the mere translator between them.

"Your mother liked birds, didn't she?" asked Mary.

"Yeah," Audrey answered softly.

"I thought so." Audrey turned to glance at the grave behind her, and Mary immediately sensed her sadness. "Like Mrs. Grant, I don't know where your mother is now either. But I do remember she loved to read stories to you. I remember she enjoyed riding bicycles and making decorations out of things she found in the woods. Mrs. Grant is real in a different way. But your mother can be real as long as you never stop remembering her. She doesn't have to be a ghost for you to be with her."

"Thanks. I should've known that."

"When you want to be with her, just close your eyes and *remember*. That's what I do."

"What do you mean?"

"Well, I've been here a while. So many seasons I've lost count. Bluebell's not my first friend. After a while . . . Well, they just can't seem to keep up with me anymore."

Mary made complete sense to Audrey. And Mary felt she understood Audrey as well. Ever since that morning in mid-June when Audrey realized Mary was more than what she seemed, being with her gave her a sense of comfort. And now, actually *speaking* with her, the feeling ran deeper. For the first time since her mother had died, she was overcome with peace. Solace.

Audrey reached in her pocket and produced a cellophane package filled with small gumballs. She ripped open the package and placed an orange ball in her mouth. "I love bubblegum," she said. "I even have my own gumball machine in my room."

"I don't know what it is," Mary confessed, eyeing the multicolored balls.

"Well, you just chew it. Your jaw gets sore after a while, and you have to spit it out, but it tastes good. Watch this." Audrey first chewed in little bites. Her eyebrows lifted higher and higher as she then stuck out her tongue with the sticky substance wrapped around it. Mary watched in amazement as Audrey then blew out through her mouth, creating an orange bubble that grew out of her lips and covered the front of her face. It reminded her of the frogs along the river, how their throats would puff up when they spoke. The bubble continued to grow, until finally, it exploded over Audrey's chin and nose. Audrey laughed as she peeled it from her face. Mary laughed too.

"Can you taste?" asked Audrey.

"I don't know."

"Here." Audrey took the gum out of her mouth. She reached up and placed the wet wad between Mary's lips. "Can you taste anything?"

Mary thought for a moment. "I don't think so, but leave it there a while. Maybe I will eventually." Mary tried to blow a breathless bubble. "I can't make it grow on my face like you did, Audrey. I can't even breathe," she sighed.

"You *don't* have to breathe. You *don't* have to eat. You're going to live forever!" Audrey marveled as she moved to paint the backside of her robe. Audrey realized humans were weak. They could get hurt, become sick and old. They could die. But Mary—she was indestructible. None of those things would ever happen to her. In Mary, she found someone who would never leave, someone who would never abandon her.

But Mary saw it differently. Many years had passed since she had been created. And while she had never once regretted her existence, she knew forever was a long time. More than she would admit, even to herself, she feared slowly eroding and eventually melting into dust. And she often wondered when she finally *did* turn to dust, would it be over? After the transition, would she become like Audrey's mother—alive only in memories? Or would she still be herself, just scattered across the ground in tiny particles, finally able to travel about the earth by riding the wind?

"Looks like you've got yourself a devotee, a regular fan," Jesus shouted down to Mary.

She smiled. "I suppose I do," she said. "And I suppose you're jealous?"

"*Jealous?* Huh? I don't understand," said Audrey, confused.

"Mrs. Grant! You didn't have to repeat that! I was talking to Jesus," explained Mary.

Mrs. Grant stood, perturbed. "I've had a bit too much of this besides the fact. You've both wasted enough time. If you all want to continue living in a dump, then fine with me. I was just trying to help by talking to the girl," she said, folding her arms and pursing her lips.

"Wait! I should at least introduce her to the others," said Mary.

"Oh, never mind that! I'll do it myself. You'll take all day." Mrs. Grant rose several feet off the ground and pointed to the top of the hill. "That's Jesus," she said hastily. Audrey shielded her eyes from the morning sun and smiled up at him. Mrs. Grant then spun in the opposite direction and flailed her wrist towards the crypt as if she were shooing a fly. "And those two, that's Arthur and that's Gareth."

"Nice to meet you." Audrey bowed her head a bit, unsure of the proper etiquette when meeting statues. "I promise I'll clean you all. Somehow, I'll get the cemetery back to normal."

"Well talk is cheap, my dear. Why don't you step it up and finish with that robe if you two insist on such rubbish? And after that, get that dried egg off Gareth's face," ordered Mrs. Grant. "He looks bad enough without it." Gareth produced a smooching sound, which ended with a loud *smack!* Mrs. Grant shuddered with disgust. "If only I had a bridge to jump off," she muttered.

After Audrey finished the last fold in Mary's robe, she stepped back to the edge of the platform to view her work. The blue garment covered almost all of Mary's body, from her base to her shoulders. She left her head covering white, and the contrast of the naturally pale stone against the vibrant blue paint was striking. She beamed with pride. Mary was truly radiant. "It's done!" she announced to Mary, pleased with the gift she had given her friend.

"What the hell is going on!" Audrey spun around, still clutching the near-empty can of paint. Her father charged out of the forest. He moved towards her in large strides, his open shirt waving to his sides. She dropped the can. It hit the edge of the platform and rolled near her mother's grave. "What have you done!" he screamed. She frantically looked for support, but Mrs. Grant was gone, silencing Mary and breaking her connection with the others. Before she had a chance to process the intensity of the moment, he grabbed her by the shoulders and pulled her from the platform. She squirmed in his grip, pressing her palms into his chest. The paint on her hands smeared blue across his skin.

"She *asked* me to do it!" she bawled. "She *wanted* a blue robe!"

It sickened him, the site of Mary in a spray-painted robe, gum stuck to her face. He scanned the rest of the defiled cemetery, unable to fathom why his daughter would do such a thing. "You let me down. You let your mother down," he said in a tone so grim it made Audrey's stomach ache. She could have protested further, but didn't see the use. She had already been found guilty, and her explanation would've sounded preposterous.

He gripped her wrist and dragged her out of the cemetery. Audrey fought as long as she could to keep Mary in view. Mary watched in agony—until he pulled her into the trees. She was greatly pained by the sound of her sobbing. The unbearable cries were silenced only when he had her behind the walls of the house.

Audrey was immediately barred to her room, where she stood in front of her window, gazing to the cemetery. Mary, obscured by the trees, was nothing more than a faint collection of blue speckles. Still, even from afar, they felt a connection. Each understood how strongly she had affected the other. In Mary's sense of the word, they began to *worship*— each other.

8

BLUEBELL

A car door slammed shut, awaking Bluebell in the bushes. The dense shrubbery he burrowed in had kept him safe and warm while he slept away from his familiar home. Sunlight poked through the tiny leaves. He was happy to see light. It provided him much needed comfort after the dark and tumultuous events of the night before. He chirped quietly as he smelled the morning air. Although his left wing ached, rest had diminished much of the pain he had endured from Greg's blow.

He had escaped the cemetery by dizzily flying through the darkness. He hated abandoning Mary, but he was frightened and didn't want to risk being struck again. Furthermore, he had no doubt that Mrs. Grant could effectively scare off the teens. Yet escaping became only his first objective. Once he was a safe distance from the chaos, he found himself flying with purpose, with determination. He found himself flying past his comfortable home in the wooden fence. He flew across town, vowing to himself to return to Mary the next day. This time, finally with some concrete information. He knew Mary well. After what she and the others had endured, he knew she would crave answers more than ever—answers that he figured were well deserved. She had placed such faith in humans only to see it rewarded with violence and destruction. The humans, they owed it to Mary, he reasoned.

He squeezed his way through the tightly-woven mass of tiny leaves and branches and cocked his head to the sky. The roof reached higher than most of the surrounding trees, culminating in a dramatic peak. He flew up the steep slope and perched atop the building. The church was set apart from the town. To get there, the townspeople had to take a series of short dirt roads. He eyed them coming in from the dusty parking lot. The ladies were colorful in their summer dresses. The men, mostly farmers and factory workers who typically wore jeans or overalls, looked distinguished in their dress pants and ties. He wondered why they bothered with the fuss of putting on such clothes, especially with all the dust swirling in the air.

He waited for the right moment. He knew if he was to ever gather information of any significance, he must find his way inside. So when the bell behind him began to ring, he dove from the roof. To stable his entry, he circled the parking lot and then headed boldly for the door. But despite his courage, Bluebell, being timid by nature, suddenly became frightened—frightened of all the people, frightened of being trapped in the enclosed space he was fast approaching. Unable to override his instincts, he quickly veered to the side of the church, scarcely landing on one of the rocks that jutted out from the building. He used the rocks as steps and lightly flapped his wings to climb from one to the next until he reached one of the three narrow, yet tall windows. He peered inside. His heart sank as he watched the Strange Man's two helpers pull shut the tall double doors, cementing his failure.

He knew the rest of the routine. The townspeople quickly filed in from the foyer, filling the long wooden benches. Some knelt and made a peculiar gesture before taking a seat down the row. A woman grabbed her young son, who was chasing two girls. The girls giggled as they found their way to their seats. The Strange Man, who had been greeting people in the foyer, was the last to come inside. He stepped upon the stage and thumbed through his book behind the lectern. He wore his usual dark robe with a speck of white showing from under his collar. Behind him stood a giant wooden cross. Bluebell had seen them before—the ones made of stone in the cemetery, of course, but he also saw them alongside roads. He'd perch atop them to eye bugs in the tall weeds. Yet the cross in the Ruthsford church was the largest he had ever seen.

The Strange Man cleared his throat. "First off, I'd like to take this time to congratulate Frank and Beth Windall on the birth of their third child. It's true that birth is the most blessed event." He nodded to the couple. "And Beth has told me they have chosen *Noah*, a quite meaningful name from scripture. I'm sure you're all as pleased with their choice as I am. I only hope when little Noah grows up, he will come to realize the significance of his namesake."

Bluebell eyed the other Mary. Besides having the same face, there were many differences between this Mary and the Mary he knew. She was much smaller. Her hands were clasped before her instead of outstretched. And most peculiar, this Mary had no body. Her waist melted into the pillar she sat atop. Bluebell never relayed this information. He thought Mary would be horrified to think of a disfigured statue that resembled her. He also did not tell her that this Mary had color. He worried she'd be envious of the flesh-like tones of her face, and the light blue covering over her head. Blue, he knew, was her favorite color. It was agonizing to think of the knowledge the *inside Mary* was certain to possess. But with him outside, she might as well have been a million miles away.

"Now!" the Strange Man's voice boomed. "Turn to Revelation, Chapter 16." His stern voice no longer matched the ever-present smile he displayed. "This is it folks! This is when the judgment of each and every one of you will take place. And it's not gonna matter who you are, where you come from, or how much money you have. It's simply not gonna matter!" He raised his hands, let his sleeves fall back, and then pushed the rim of his glasses up his nose. "'And there were voices, and thunders, and lightnings. And there was a great earthquake, such as was not since men were upon the earth. So mighty an earthquake. And so great!' This folks, is just a taste of it. This folks—is Armageddon. And it's coming. Doubt not!"

Suddenly, a blinding flash of light shot across the room. "Sweet Jesus!" a lady called out. The Strange Man stopped abruptly and shielded his eyes. The crowd spun to look at the dark figures standing inside the doorway with the morning sun burning behind them. Slowly, the doors creaked shut again, and the light disappeared until it was only a sliver that ran down the center of the aisle.

"I'm sorry," a deep voice muttered. He took another step inside, embarrassed. He wore gray pants and a white dress shirt unbuttoned at the collar. His hair was freshly slicked back. He clenched her hand as they walked down the aisle, his eyes darting nervously for an open seat.

Finally recognizing them, the Strange Man nodded with approval. "Well welcome," he said. "Have a seat." Their appearance surprised them all and caused hushed whispers to break out among the crowd. It had been the first time they had appeared in the church since the funeral. Mr. Lansly promptly found them a seat in a row near the back of the room.

Audrey's yellow sundress contradicted her somber mood. She hung her head low, hiding her face behind her loose curls. She was not the same wide-eyed child Bluebell saw gushing to Mary only the day before. She seemed instead like an unhappy doll—a perfectly composed child on the outside, yet not permitted to speak of her misery.

As the priest cleared his throat and continued, Audrey slowly began to acknowledge her surroundings. It wasn't often she found herself inside the church, and the expansive ceiling and ornate decorations begged her eyes to explore. She tilted her neck backward and gazed to the high beams of the ceiling. She watched the rotating fans that seemed to jut a bit too precariously from such a height. Unable to sit still, she next swiveled to face the back of the church. She stood upon her knees to look to the balcony above the massive doors.

Her father grabbed her arm and forced her to sit properly. "Sit still!" he whispered firmly in her ear. He wanted their presence to be normal. He wanted them to be accepted. He knew he had to do *something* to keep her from spinning out of control again, and he had hope in the church. He brought her there with the thought that more exposure to the church, to its people, might help stave off any future extreme outbursts of sacrilege.

Audrey, of course, quickly minded her father and became attentive to the priest. Yet it was easy to become lost in his droning voice; and after a while, she only pretended to listen. Instead, she focused on the small statue of Mary positioned on a pillar beside the pulpit.

Bluebell watched as Audrey's lips moved in silent messages to the other Mary. Were they communicating? If so, he desperately wanted to hear what they were saying. He felt foolish being outside, straining to hear. He *needed* to find a way in! Frustrated, he strutted back and forth across the ledge, pressing his body against the glass.

The attention Audrey had placed on the statue was quickly diverted. Outside one of the windows, on the opposite side of the church, the movement of something blue caught her eye. She was shocked to see that it was a bird—a bluebird—the same tiny bluebird that Mary had been desperately missing! She immediately stood. "Bluebell!" she shouted. The entire congregation turned to face her in unison. The priest stopped, interrupted once again. Bluebell became still on the ledge, shocked that Audrey knew his name. "You're alive!" she declared. She trampled over others' feet as she ran across the church to the window. "Mary's worried about you! You have to go back to the cemetery!" She cupped her hands around her mouth to assure he could hear her through the glass. "Go back to Mary!" she shouted.

Her father stood with a mix of rage and embarrassment. "Audrey, sit down!"

"Dad, he *has* to go back to the cemetery! It's our fault he left his home. We're responsible for whatever happened to him there!"

"*You're* responsible," he said sternly.

She ran down the main aisle and tugged open the massive double doors. "Go back!" she shouted to the rising sun.

"That's enough, Audrey!"

She stood silent with her back to the crowd as she raised her arms in anticipation, hoping to see him fly into the sun. The parishioners too watched in a hushed stillness, wondering what would happen next. And soon, the bird *did* fly in front of the building. Yet just as he looked as if he would fly off into the horizon as Audrey had instructed, he altered his direction and began to make his way towards the church.

Seizing the opportunity, Bluebell flew through the open doors, over Audrey's outstretched arms, and headed for the pulpit. A collective gasp came from the congregation as he circled the unsuspecting priest and landed on the other Mary's head. "Mary! Mary! Talk to me!" Bluebell chirped desperately, trying to find footing on her smooth head. "There's more like you! You have to help! You can let others know what you know!" His chirping grew louder. "Wake up! Wake up!" Yet despite his frantic efforts, her face remained cold. She did not seem to have a voice.

A thin, elderly lady adjusted her mesh hat before picking up a broom that leaned against the wall. She used it to swat at Bluebell, nearly hitting him. "Shoo!" she yelled at him. Bluebell fluttered above her. As she took another swing, he became so frightened, he let go of a dropping. It landed atop her head and oozed through the mesh and into her white hair. She dropped the broom and ran disgusted and embarrassed to the restroom. A stern-looking woman with short red hair promptly took her place. She grabbed the broom, and was able to reach it even higher. Bluebell lifted himself near the top of the ceiling, near the fans. Afraid of the spinning blades, he circled below them in tiring rotations.

"Stop that!" Audrey shouted. She ran to the woman and yanked the broom from her hands. She smacked the woman's shins with the straw end of the broom, scolding her.

"Audrey!" her father yelled over the commotion. He stood on the opposite end of the center aisle. His face was flushed.

His hands trembled with fury and shame. "Come here—now!" he demanded.

She approached him reluctantly, dragging the broom behind her. As she came closer, he bent down with open arms as if he was about to give her a hug. But instead, he scooped her up and tossed her over his shoulder. The broom handle smacked against the floor as she let go of her grip. And as he carried her limp body through the doors, Audrey made one final attempt to help Bluebell: she reached for the wall and flipped off the switch that controlled the ceiling fans. He carried her out of the church, not bothering to apologize.

9
THE TRUTH

Bluebell found safety tucked in a concealed corner of the rafters. Stuck high in the ceiling, all he could think of was Mary. He reasoned she must've been so worried that she somehow found a way to communicate his disappearance to young Audrey, triggering her outburst. He peered down at the other Mary, who was useless, empty. His efforts, and the despair he had caused his good friend, were in vain.

"Well, we've had quite an eventful morning to say the least, haven't we?" the Strange Man said. The crowd answered with uneasy murmurs. Bluebell was relieved when the man decided to dismiss them early. They left the church in huddled groups of conversation. He waited patiently, until the whispering voices faded and the whirs of their engines were replaced by the soft rush of the wind that rolled over the roof. He waited until the Strange Man himself and his helpers exited the room through a door beside the stage.

Cautiously, he poked out of the corner. When he was sure the room was empty, he swooped down from the ceiling. He spread his wings and sailed just above the benches, circling the room. The double doors had been sealed, and the door the

Strange Man disappeared into was also shut. He circled again. The brightness of outside attracted him. He landed on the sill of one of the gigantic windows and pushed against the glass, flapping with all his might. The invisible barrier was cruel. It allowed him to clearly see freedom, while effectively keeping him from it.

"You cannot leave!" a feminine, yet firm voice echoed throughout the room.

Startled, Bluebell flew from the window and landed atop the massive wooden cross. "*Mary?*" he questioned as he eyed the lone statue. Now that the room had become empty and silent, had *her* silence finally been broken? "You're not just stone?" he wondered.

"What 'tis your name?" she asked, while at the same time answering his question.

"Bluebell."

"I see you often, Bluebell, looking in from the windows. Why have *you*, a creature from the outside, taken such an interest in this church? In a statue such as myself?" Her voice sounded different from the humans and the other statues he knew. It sounded more formal, more sophisticated. It made Bluebell feel slightly intimidated.

"There are others," he said, and then swallowed nervously. He pointed the tip of his wing towards the window. "Beyond the forest. Perhaps more beyond that."

"Yes, I know it to be true," she sighed.

"That's why I came to you, Mary."

"My name is not Mary."

"Of course it is. What else could it be?"

"My name is Alice."

"*Alice?* How can it be—"

"You have informed me that you have a name, correct?"

"Absolutely!" Bluebell proudly stuck out his chest, remembering the day he had been named.

"Your name is not *Bird*, is it?"

"No."

"Of course not. It 'tis Bluebell. My name is not Mary, it 'tis Alice. I *am* a Mary. However, my *name* is Alice."

"Well I know a Mary whose *name* is Mary too. That's who I'm here for."

"How thoughtful of you to have traveled on her behalf. However, I must confess, I do not understand why she would send you here—to see *me*."

"Because she needs your help—and so do the others!" Bluebell stopped himself, realizing he was not above his own mission. "We *all* do," he confessed.

"And how do you propose I help you and your friends?"

"You could give me a message—a message containing your knowledge, and I will bring it back to Mary and the others."

"But such a message; it would be void, for I have no message to send."

"But Mary—I mean *Alice*, you *must* know more than us from being inside—inside the church with the humans and the Strange Man they all listen to!"

"Perhaps. But I assure you, whatever knowledge that has been imparted upon me by the humans is merely hearsay."

"Then it wouldn't trouble you if I asked a few questions?"

"Judging by today's events, Bluebell, you have obviously piqued the humans' interest. I cannot deny you have done the same to me. You may proceed."

His first question, he asked for Mary. It was crude, yet he knew it had to be asked, for reassurance if nothing else. He asked it swiftly, hoping Alice wouldn't be offended. "Are statues alive?"

"We certainly must be!" she answered immediately. "Otherwise I would not be talking to you, now would I?"

"No, I suppose not."

"However," she regained her calmness, "that is not to say just because a thing does not speak means it 'tis without life. *Speaking* is not the only evidence to be considered to prove or disprove life. Trees are alive. Grass is alive. Even some buildings are alive. Why this church, it 'tis alive!"

"What about ghosts?"

"*Ghosts?*"

"Yes. I know of a ghost named Mrs. Grant. She is with the others in the cemetery."

Alice thought for a moment. "Yes. She is alive too."

"How can she be alive if she's—well—she's dead!"

"She is not dead. She merely exists in an in-between stage."

"An *in-between stage?*"

"That 'tis correct. You see, Bluebell, we are in a stage right now. Your ghost-friend, Mrs. Grant, for whatever reason was not ready to advance to her next stage, so now she must reside in her present form until she is ready."

"Ready for what?"

Alice laughed delicately. "There is no way for me to know. It 'tis different for each one. We are *all* waiting to move onto the next stage, but we mustn't dwell on it. It will come to her, to us, naturally. When our spirit is ready to move on, then so shall we. We will go to the soft light. It will warm us. It will comfort us."

Bluebell thought of the sun warming him in the morning. "Then what?" he shrugged and then shook his tail feathers, eagerly awaiting her answer.

"Some humans believe that one then returns in the form of another human, or perhaps an animal, which in my opinion demonstrates what a limited view they have. Others believe that one stays in the light until the end of time. I, on the other hand, have always believed it depends on where one's spirit *chooses* to go."

"One's *spirit?*" The short feathers on the back of his neck stood up. As far as Bluebell was aware, the topics they discussed had never been discussed before. He felt privileged being able to talk with Alice, privileged to hear her secrets.

"A spirit is what makes everything living—alive!" she explained.

"Like a *soul?*"

"Exactly!"

Bluebell impressed even himself with his use of the term he had acquired from his many visits to the church's window. "But I thought souls—spirits—were only in *them.*" He gazed over the empty benches.

Alice needn't a moment to think before she replied, "Spirits are not exclusive to humans. *You* have a spirit, Bluebell."

"Does Mary have a spirit?"

"Of course she has. And so too do cats and cornstalks. *Everything* that 'tis alive has a spirit."

"Where do our spirits come from?"

"I must confess, I cannot say."

"But you *must* know. The humans are the ones with the answers. Certainly, you've heard it from them."

"Oh Bluebell," she laughed. "The truth is humans do not know any more about their existence than either you or I. Do you think I have come about my view of this world by solely listening to the speeches in this church? Heavens no! I have not always been here, you see. I was created in a land called England on the other side of a vast ocean. Throughout many years, I have traveled from church to church; I was even outside in a public square for some time. And while the humans *have* given me insight, I have gained just as much knowledge from speaking with mice traveling along floorboards, from listening to flocks of birds passing overhead, even from observing the rising sun. Humans, they may speculate as we. They may conjure their ideas, but they do not know."

"They know God," Bluebell interjected, stamping his feet on the cross.

"They know God as the creator of all things great and small. They do not *know* God."

"Then the humans—they are like us?" marveled Bluebell.

"Closer than you think."

Bluebell sailed from the cross and landed on the outer armrest of the pew nearest Alice. He had learned so much from her in such a short time. He could barely contain it in his head. "I must tell Mary!" he said anxiously. He knew his discoveries would fascinate her. "Thank you for your help, Alice," he said, bowing to her in gratitude.

"Are you leaving?" she asked.

"Yes, I must go now," he said, looking to the windows. The sky had already begun to darken. "But I hope to visit again if that's alright?" He hoped they would become friends, and that through him, she would become friends with the others as well.

"You cannot leave! Not so soon!"

"You have given me plenty of information for the time being, and now I must return to the cemetery and share what you have taught me. You see, I am just a bird, and I can only hold onto so much—"

"But you cannot leave!"

"But I must! You heard the little girl—Mary, she's worried about me! I can't allow her to suffer much longer."

"I gave you knowledge, did I not? The least you could do is entertain my company," she said, full of spite. She then took a moment to compose a softer, yet pleading tone. "How I wish I was outside again, Bluebell. Your friend, Mary, she can easily find another bird. But it could be years before I find another worthy companion under this roof."

"Tell me how I can leave!" he persisted.

"The doors, the windows—they are all sealed. There *is* no way out. But never mind that, Bluebell. We have much more to talk about! We can discuss anything you fancy. It would be my honor. Surely, you have many more questions. There *must* be more."

"Of course there's more," he admitted. "But—"

"Then it 'tis settled. You shall remain with me in exchange for my thoughts, and through the course, we will make fine companions."

Bluebell looked through the nearest window. Beyond the parking lot was a large willow tree among a field of goldenrods and Queen Anne's lace. He could tell by the way the willow's limbs swayed that a storm was brewing. Even so, he longed to be outside, to be free. He pictured the large leaves of the oak tree in the cemetery; he thought of the cool water of the river as he flapped his wings against the invisible glass.

10
THE STORM

After nearly a week without rain, darkness etched its way back into the Ruthsford sky causing the afternoon to prematurely turn to evening. The weak summer breezes gathered strength, pushing against the window panes and rattling the metal eaves troughs. The trees creaked and swayed as the gushing wind swirled around the house and up through their limbs. It forced its way between the leaves and pine needles, making it sound as if there were a giant vacuum outside. The occasional drops of rain began to increase along with the wind's force until both began to pound the house. Distant flashes of light followed deep rumblings.

Audrey lay on her stomach with her arms over the end of the bed, stretching to reach her drawing tablet. Colored pencils were strewn across the floor. She carefully chose a shade of gray and began to slowly move the pencil back and forth. She stared intently at the tip as it transferred the dull shade to the paper. She easily became lost in the movements, yet couldn't ignore the dark lines that bled through from the page beneath. She was well aware of the image that begged to be seen. She had been resisting the urge to look, but eventually found herself setting her pencil aside and lifting the page for a quick look at the watercolor portrait of her father. She and her mother had taken turns painting it. She remembered giggling as he squirmed in his seat, teasing her about how long it was taking to complete.

"Am I in the right light?" he joked, bringing his face in front of the desk lamp she had clipped to the table to better illuminate his features.

"When Audrey and I are done with you, you'll be hanging in a gallery," she recalled her mother joking. "There, I've finished with his eyes. Audrey, why don't you shade them like I've shown you? Then you can start on his nose."

Audrey examined the raw painting. A rippled streak ran through the center of his face where she had spilled a cup of dirty paint water. And although one ear was larger than the other and the nose was no more than an upside-down question mark, the face was unmistakably her father's. The wrinkles of his forehead were there. So too were his tufts of dark hair and boyish smile. Even his usual light stubble had been captured, created by the tapping of sharp bristles. Seeing the portrait only reminded her of the strain between them.

The ride home from church was silent, yet filled with his disappointment. She let her mind escape the truck by concentrating on the dark clouds that rolled in from the distant horizon. The sky echoed her despair. They drove towards it, and eventually met the darkness at the house. He stopped at the end of the driveway, and she let herself out of the pick-up. "I'm going into town," he said solemnly before speeding away. She walked up the drive alone, unsure of when he'd return.

She flipped back to her drawing, and her father's face was replaced with a scene of the cemetery. It was quite detailed, complete with Jesus towering atop a hill of gravestones, a crypt with cat-like creatures above either side of the door, and power lines draped over a turquoise river. There was a tree with individually-drawn leaves. Looped onto one of the branches was a knotted rope, from which a white-haired woman in a purple gown dangled. And though the sky was full of gray clouds, a lone beam of sun broke through, illuminating the woman who stood in the center. The woman wore a vibrant blue dress, and on her shoulder sat a bird of the same shade. In the drawing, Mary's radiance was eternal.

The lightning no longer came in distant flashes, but in visible streaks. Audrey stood from her bed. She approached the window with apprehension, nervously smoothing out the wrinkles in the yellow dress she still wore. As the next bolt penetrated the sky, she leapt backwards onto a colored pencil, snapping it in two. She took a deep breath before bravely stepping to the window once more. Each flash of light allowed her to catch a glimpse of the gravestones beyond the trees. Even with the rain and lightning, Audrey wished she could've been in the cemetery with Mary. She wanted to tell her that she had seen Bluebell—that he was alive. But she was afraid of her father, afraid he'd catch her in the cemetery after forbidding her to enter.

She opened the window and welcomed the forceful air inside. The clean scents from the wet trees and wildflowers immediately filled the room. The wind forced the rain inside. It fell on her toes and soaked the carpet. With the window open, the thunder was even louder, closer. It growled like a deep, evil voice. "Audrey," it called to her. She was confused. There was static and other voices. "Audrey," it said again with more clarity. "Audrey!" The bedroom door flew open. She spun around. Rain sprayed the back of her dress.

Her father stood before her. He too was still in his Sunday clothes, yet they were so drenched they clung to his skin. Clipped to his belt was a small transistor radio. Through the static, a voice said, "—and we're expecting more heavy winds and rain throughout the remainder of tonight and into tomorrow." He stumbled towards her, and the voice was obscured by crackles.

"It's coming," he said, almost out of breath. "The river—it's going to flood." His eyes were glazed over and red. "I was just out there. It's rising too fast—halfway up the bank. We have to stop it!"

"We *can't* stop it," Audrey whispered, afraid.

"Your mother's out there!" he reminded her.

He stood upright, and the radio came back to life. A series of short beeps sounded, followed by a message from the announcer: "The National Weather Service has issued a severe thunderstorm warning as well as a flash flood warning for Ottawa county . . ."

He turned down the volume and offered his hand to her. "Let's go!" he said. Audrey reluctantly took his hand, and he rushed her down the hall. "I picked these up for you in town," he said as they neared the back door. Audrey was unsure of what he referred to until he lifted the pair of black boots from the doormat and handed them to her. They resembled men's combat boots, but in a child's size. And seeing them, she knew then she was truly going to war. She thrust the boots over her bare feet, trying to convey urgency, which she knew he would require. The yellow dress and the high boots that met it would become her battle fatigues; and it would do no good trying to convince her commanding officer to turn around. It was too late. He was too determined. The soft eyes and wry smile of his portrait were replaced by a manic, yet focused look. He was simply not the same man.

He led her outside. She did not bother to grab her coat, nor did he. Lightning flashed, and Audrey saw the pick-up waiting. It had been backed up to the house, the engine still running. He took out his flashlight and motioned for her to look in the bed of the truck—at the weapons they'd be using. Audrey watched as his light caressed the stacks of white sandbags that overflowed the bed of the truck. "Got them at the gravel pits," he grinned. He pointed the beam of light up the muddy driveway for a moment and then stepped inside the cab. Audrey followed his lead, promptly taking her position beside him.

He flashed on the lights, and raindrops popped in front of the beams like a television tuned to static. The windshield wipers squeaked back and forth with ferocity, but were only able to provide intermittent glimpses of visibility. The engine growled and steam rose from the hood as they rolled down the driveway and turned onto the main road. Sections of gravel were gone completely, washed away by massive pools of muddy water. It looked to Audrey as if a giant cup of weak coffee had been spilled over the road. The unrelenting drops of rain exploded on the water's surface and were then absorbed, causing the giant pools to grow larger before their eyes. The tires disappeared beneath the deep water. Yet undeterred, he kept the truck at a steady speed, hoping to prevent it from becoming stuck.

Suddenly, he jerked the steering wheel sharply to the right, and Audrey was lifted from her seat. She grasped the dash as the truck lurched off the road and onto the two-track with a bounce. The mud on the two-track was much darker, thicker than on the main road. It oozed between the tread of the tires. Wet branches hung low on either side, making the path ahead a cramped tunnel. As they moved forward, leaves stuck to the windows like pressing hands; branches scraped across the body of the truck like giant claws trying to force them to retreat. The sounds alone were maddening.

As Audrey clutched the hand grip, she looked to her father. His face was contorted in battle. He leaned forward with his hands clenching the steering wheel. He *was* in a war—a war against the elements of nature. He fought the darkness, the trees and rain. Yet as the truck finally met the end of the organic tunnel, as the scratching claws weakened their grip, he grinned with assured triumph.

The truck sped into the clearing and barreled down the hill. Audrey couldn't tell if he was in control, or if he simply guided the truck as one would a sled careening down a slippery hill. They slid to a stop at the bottom—just inches away from the first row of headstones where the path began to loop. "Damn right!" he shouted excitedly over his impressive feat.

He relaxed his grip on the steering wheel a bit as they moved slowly along the gravel path. Audrey watched as the headlights cast moving shadows of the graves over the soggy earth. They passed the oak tree. Soaked toilet paper still clung to it, concealing its green beauty. They passed Mrs. Grant's graffiti-filled crypt. They passed her mother's plot. And they passed Mary. Audrey eyed the faint blue stream that trickled down her platform. Slowly, she lifted her hand to the window in an uneasy greeting. She fought her instincts and remained silent. She didn't let on how desperately she needed him to stop the truck.

"It's already too high from last month's rain," he said as they approached the bank. "Talk down at the tavern is that the river could easily flood the low-lying areas by morning. The graves up the hill should be fine. But below . . ." He opened his door and stuck out his head as he slowly backed the truck up to the bank. They jerked to a halt just a few feet from the rising water. "Let's do it for her," he said hauntingly.

Audrey looked to the cemetery before her. There was Mary, bright and blue. The headlights shined on her like spotlights. Surely, her father wasn't speaking of *her*. She stood tall enough and far enough away that it would take weeks, perhaps months of steady rain to even reach the bottom of her robe. But of course, Audrey knew it was not Mary he spoke of. Even still, her mother's grave seemed reasonably safe. She could not fathom the water rising all the way to the center of the cemetery, no matter how heavy the rain or how violent the storm.

She heard the tailgate creak open before she realized he had even left the cab. She quickly jumped out of the truck and ran beside him. "Start on that side," he directed immediately. "I'll start over there, and we'll close off this entire area." He waved his hand, illustrating the large gap between the trees along the bank. He then grabbed a sandbag in each arm. He carried them to his side of the bank and heaved them into the mud near the waterline.

Audrey chose a sandbag close to the edge of the tailgate. She tugged on its corners, and when it began to slide off the edge, she quickly made a cradle with her arms and let it fall. Carefully, she edged herself along the riverbank, hoping the traction her boots provided was enough to support her and the heavy bag. Her hair, quickly drenched by the rain, stuck to her face and covered her eyes. Her dress clung to her like the wet toilet paper on the oak tree. She carefully positioned herself before letting the sandbag plop to the mud. The wet mixture of mud and clay sprayed up from the ground, covering her yellow dress. Freed of the extra weight, she lost her balance and slipped backwards. Her legs slid into the rushing water. She thrust herself forward and crawled onto the bank only to see her father standing over her. "We have to beat it, Audrey!" He handed her another sandbag before she had a chance fully regain her stance.

He moved madly to and from the bank, furiously stacking the bags with all his strength, fear and anger. Audrey's small frame could not match his power, but she tried to match his zeal. She mocked him, in a way, with each sandbag she tirelessly slapped to the mud. And when her arms became weak and her lungs exhausted, she pushed herself even further. If she collapsed, maybe then he would see what he was doing to her.

After half the bags were in position, he stood back and examined their work. He held his hands to his hips and shook his head. "Goddamn it! It's not working!" he shouted. He marched up to Audrey. "We don't have enough bags! The water—it's still rising!" He wiped the rain from his forehead. "We're going to have to move her!" he hollered over the wind.

"*Move her?*"

"She's going to drown otherwise!"

She looked into his wild eyes, but did not question him. She was too frightened by the sincerity in his voice. "What do you want me to do?" she asked instantly.

He placed his hand on her shoulder. "You stay here and finish the bank. I'll take care of your mother." As he grabbed a shovel from the back of the pick-up, a bolt of lightning struck over the hill, capturing the moment like an enormous camera flash. For that second, it was brighter than day. Audrey stood frozen for a moment, absorbing the shockwave of light and noise that ran through her body. The impression of her father holding the shovel amid the gravestones remained in her vision long after the darkness had returned.

He dug with fierceness. The waterlogged ground was heavy. It stubbornly held its place, but it seemed little could interfere with his strength, his determination that night. In a short time, he had uncovered six inches, then a foot. After each shovelful, he came closer to freeing her from her wet prison.

Wind swirled around Audrey. It cooled her skin as it blew against the mixture of sweat and water. She opened her mouth with thirst, letting the rainwater collect on her tongue. She then closed her eyes for a moment. She thought of just what her father was uncovering. And then thought of Mary's words. It was true. There *was* no way of knowing what had happened to her mother, where she had gone after her death. Yet Audrey was certain she would not be found inside the empty body that lay beneath the earth. Just like a gravestone was an inadequate substitute for her mother, so too was her body. Mary had been right. The only way to keep her alive was to remember the way she was, not to preserve the flesh she had abandoned. For the first time, Audrey admitted to herself that her father was simply wrong. He could've shoveled all night amidst the violent bolts of light, but it wouldn't have mattered. He dug in vain.

Another flash shot down from the sky. It sounded like a cannon as it struck a pine tree on the other side of the river, splitting its trunk. The tree toppled to the ground, burning. Audrey spun to watch the faint orange glow flicker through the mass of trees. She then lifted her head to view the clouds above. They painted the sky a swirling sea of black. And in front of this backdrop streaked strands of white light. The sky was electric, powerful. "It's overhead!" she called to him.

He noticed her shouting, but could not hear her over the roaring wind. He grinned and waved to her as if he were simply a parent watching a child from across a playground. In spite of the storm's overwhelming power, his progress was impressive. His legs were mostly hidden beneath the earth as he stood in the trench he had created. This made him look all the more peculiar when he gripped the shovel over his head and shook it towards the sky in an exuberant, yet disturbing display of triumph. After lowering the shovel, he motioned for Audrey to continue her work along the bank.

They were heavy, but she managed to tuck one sandbag under each arm as her father had. She concentrated on the movements of her legs, whispering "right, left" to herself as she placed one foot in front of the other. She carefully made her way to the river and then turned her back to it to lay down the first bag. She used her boot to kick it into place, and automatically slid into the river up to her knees. Undaunted, she dropped the other bag and pounded it into place with her fist while still in the water. She then pulled herself out of the river and stood among the barrier she had created.

Water inched its way up, forming tiny pools and tiny rivers in the crevices between the bags. Suddenly, the clay shelf that supported her crumbled. It broke into the current, sending the sandbags splashing to the bottom of the river. Audrey too plunged backwards and splashed under the water. For a moment, she was completely submerged, and then, she bobbed to the surface.

The sensation of having her feet on solid ground one moment and being immersed in water the next shocked her initially. But then, she became calm. Somehow, in the midst of the storm, the river remained peaceful. She allowed herself to float and focus on the vast night sky. She felt a part of it, a part of the endless nature that surrounded her. And this feeling, this knowledge of being a part of something much larger than herself, released her from her father's demands, from the burdens he had placed upon her. And what's more, in that moment, she *understood* his emotions. She realized he couldn't help himself from having them. They were all he knew. All he could experience. She forgave him. And felt only peace.

Mary saw the next bolt reach out. It struck the transformer atop the wooden pole. Sparks shot out as one of the lines broke loose. It gracefully swung through the air and then slapped against the water. Audrey lunged forward, her body involuntarily trying to escape, but her back remained glued to the water—confined to the power of the electrical currents. The line thrashed back and forth over the surface like a snake forked to the ground. Her jaw clamped shut. Her fists tightened. Her body convulsed. Mary could see her being attacked by what looked like miniature bolts of lightning. The flashing streaks surrounded her body. Sparks flowed out of the broken line as it rose and then smacked the water again. The water—it was on fire! The peaceful river had become a lake of fire, and it was *not* glorious or beautiful. It was horrifying.

He tapped the top of the coffin with the head of his shovel and then bent over to feel the wood. The thin layer of mud that covered it was grainy to the touch. He allowed his hand to follow the extravagant flower carvings. What was once pristine had become dull and chipped. He remembered the last time he had seen the ornate carvings—the last day he had seen her. She looked ethereal, with her golden hair, laying peacefully in her white dress. "Like an angel," said Mrs. Longfellow, placing her hands at the edge of the coffin, admiring her. Everyone agreed.

The funeral to him was like a dream. So too was her death. Pushed into the far corners of his mind, it was not reality. His last *real* thought of his wife was of her bravery while being sick. She disguised her pain with smiles. So when death came for her, there were no warnings. There was no transition. She was *not* dead.

"Like an angel," he whispered as he climbed out from the grave. He wanted Audrey to be there when he freed her. He walked towards the river, overwhelmed with the thought that they were soon to be reunited as a family. "Audrey!" he called out, but did not see her along the bank. He noticed the pine burning across the river, but it did not concern him; the ground was far too wet for the flames to spread. He saw that a section of sandbags had fallen into the river. But he would not scold Audrey. The sandbags were no longer important.

"Stop him," Mary commanded as he neared the water's edge.

Mrs. Grant did not hesitate. She appeared before him with her arms folded. "I'm sorry, Mr. Lansly. But I cannot let you pass." Yet he stepped right through Mrs. Grant, unable to detect her presence. He could only focus on the yellow fabric that floated atop the water. He dashed after it, running through the trees as it drifted around the bend. "Let her go," Mrs. Grant whispered after him as she was forced to slowly fade back into the night.

Above the storm, above the trees and burning fire, a great cry was heard. It penetrated the deepest gravesite, was felt by the sheltering animals. She was caught among the dead, overhanging branches of a fallen tree. His body felt like liquid as he fell into the water. He breathed deep, yet quick breaths as he untangled her from the branches. His hand began to tremble as he brushed it against her cheek and felt her wet hair. She was like a sleeping doll, only she was *not* sleeping. She was not breathing. She was dead. *Dead.*

"What have I done!" he cried in hopeless regret. Images of her as a baby, a toddler, and as a young woman flooded his mind. He thought of their breakfasts together, their picnics along the river—and her heaving sandbags in combat boots. *Combat boots!* "Oh God!" He unlaced the boots and removed them from her feet. He threw each to the center of the river in fury. They glided with the current for a moment before sinking beneath the water.

Mary saw them emerge from the trees. She watched as he carried her lifeless body snug against his stumbling frame. For the first time in a long time, Mary closed her eyes. She pictured herself free from stone, able to help Audrey as she stacked the sandbags along the river. She imagined herself pulling Audrey out of the water well before the lightning struck the power line. But her fantasy, she found, began to only accentuate her limitations, so she quickly changed the images in her mind. She thought instead of snow. Pure. White. Peaceful snow. Yet not even the delicate flakes and cascading drifts her mind created could block the howling wind and pounding rain, which provided her free-flowing tears.

When she opened her eyes, Mr. Lansly was gone. She looked to the ground beneath her, and there, next to the grave he had uncovered, next to her mother, lay Audrey. The lights from the pick-up shined on her bare feet. They created shadows with her nose and her eyelashes. Eventually, the lights dimmed—making her and the night disappear.

11
JESUS

The rains turned to sprinkles, the winds weakened, and the monstrous streaks of power moved elsewhere. Yet the faded rumbles and the return of the gentle breezes were not comforting. There was an eeriness that came with the calm, a stillness that seemed unnatural. It was nearly morning. The sun had yet to rise, but the dim light from the horizon cast a gray hue over the cemetery.

"Is it over?" asked Jesus.

"I think so," answered Mary.

"Where's Mr. Lansly?"

"I don't know."

He strained to see her body still laying before Mary. "Is she dead?"

An awful feeling came over Mary that she hadn't felt before. It was like a ball of energy she could not release. It radiated from her stomach and rose to her throat. "Yes," she answered, sickened.

"What happens next?"

"I'm not sure. I was hoping you would tell *me* that."

"I'm frightened," he confessed.

Mary smiled briefly at his words. His honesty brought her comfort, knowing he was more like her than he cared to admit. "So am I," she offered.

Mrs. Grant could be heard weeping from inside her crypt. The gargoyles did not jeer her. "Maybe she'll be a ghost," suggested Arthur.

"Do you think she'll be a ghost, Mary? Like Mrs. Grant?" asked Gareth.

"I don't know," she answered with doubt. "Maybe."

Mrs. Grant's cries were suddenly interrupted by a deep, sinister growl. "What is *that?*" asked Mary.

Jesus used his peripheral vision to look as far as he could in the direction of the noise. "It's the tractor," he reported. "Mr. Lansly, he's in the shed."

The engine chugged slowly at first, and then began to grind powerfully as he pulled the tractor out from the small building. The massive back wheels turned steadily, denting the earth. Black smoke rose from the exhaust as he rode along the ridge of the hill. He parked the large machine just up the slope from Jesus and looked upon his cemetery—the tombstones, the statues, the serene setting he had worked so hard to maintain.

All of it was for *them*—for the visitors who came to grieve. And as the caretaker of the land, he had always sympathized with their losses, but their losses were distanced from him. No matter how many caskets he witnessed lowered underground, no matter how many times he had to say "I'm sorry," he remained unaffected by death.

He always had the feeling that because of his dedication to the dead, his family was especially protected by God. Somehow, he felt they would remain untouched. Exempt from death, or at least from a cruel and untimely demise. And why *shouldn't* his family be spared? He had protected the resting souls. He had maintained their monuments. He had chipped away at stone, carving statues in heavenly images.

For these reasons, he had long ignored the line between life and death—so much so that even after the loss of his wife, that line remained a blur. But now, after witnessing the death of his daughter, the distinction became shockingly clear. He realized he could never again hold his wife or his daughter. No longer could he protect them. His power had been taken away.

And the thought that it was *his* misinterpretation, *his* misbelief that had ultimately caused the death of his daughter—was intolerable. So it didn't take long for those feelings of guilt and regret to transform into rage. Instead of shame, he felt betrayed. Convinced he had been misled.

The anger that surged through him was born from his anguish. He was angry *because* he felt misery. It was an emotion he was never supposed to experience, an emotion he had conditioned himself not to feel. His anger came too from the loss of control, the helplessness he found accompanied death. And with this rage, he turned to God. After all he had done, *God* had taken his family from him; *God* had turned him into a miserable mourner in his own cemetery.

He let out a savage bellow and became a part of the metal beast he rode; he was in its snarl and cold metal. He focused on the icons in the cemetery: the tombstones, all that stood for God, and all that stood for death. He pulled a lever, and the lift attached to the front of the frame began to rise. He released his foot from the clutch, and the tractor jerked forward with its muscle. It barreled down the slope towards Jesus. The lift collided with his back, chipping his robe. Mr. Lansly then reversed the tractor back to its starting position. There, he stood with his foot on the clutch. "Everything!" he shouted to Jesus. "Everything you take away . . ." he said as he fell back to the seat and released the clutch once again, "I will take from you!" Once again, the powerful machine slammed into Jesus. He was lifted from his platform for a moment and then came crashing back down.

"What's happening!" shouted Mary.

Mr. Lansly slammed into him yet again. Sparks and fragments of marble flew in all directions. And with another hit, the backside of Jesus began to crumble. He became unsteady, teetering back and forth on his platform. "I'm going to fall!" he cried. With the lift pressed against his back, Mr. Lansly forced the might of the tractor upon Jesus. The wheels moved in short jerking rotations. They churned into the ground, heaving against the unstable stone.

Mary couldn't bear to hear the battle taking place behind her. Her mind raced with thoughts of how she could save him, but there was nothing she could do; there was nothing any of them could do. In desperation, she began to recite the only prayer she knew—a short poem that had taken Bluebell several trips and much recitation as he flew over the town and forest to deliver to her in its entirety. "Hail Mary full of grace. The lord is with thee . . ." she began.

The wheels spun faster, digging themselves deep into the ground; and Jesus began to tip backwards. As the tractor sunk in the muddy trench it had created, his massive weight loomed over Mr. Lansly. But the engine was strong, and Jesus' fate was soon dependent upon the outcome of his gravity versus the might of the tractor.

"Blessed art thou amongst women and blessed is the fruit of thy womb, Jesus . . ."

The tractor continued to sink. Mud from the spinning wheels splashed up his back. His own invention threatened to crush him. "I created you, Goddamn it!"

"Holy Mary, mother of God, pray for us sinners . . ."

Mr. Lansly pulled the lever, and the mechanical lift rose higher, finally tilting the colossal figure forward. Jesus looked to the horizon for the last time, and then saw the ground come closer. He crashed into the gravestones beneath. Upon impact, he heard his own torso crack. The gravestones held him suspended aboveground for only a moment before toppling under his weight. His arms instantly broke from his body, and his face dented the earth.

"Now and at the hour of our death . . ."

Mr. Lansly maneuvered the tractor out from the pit it had created, and he and the metal beast met Jesus at his side. He lowered the lift and used it to swivel his torso sideways. Then, easily rolling over the broken tombstones, he nudged him forward. Being on the steep hill, it didn't take much force before he began to roll. He looked on with satisfaction as the limbless Jesus plummeted out of control. The headstones did little to slow him. He rolled them over like bowling pins, three and four at a time, as he tumbled down the hill he once governed. He rolled into the flat portion of the cemetery and clear past the gravel path. He rolled until he reached the ground just feet before Mary.

"Amen."

She looked to Jesus. It was the first time she had seen his face. He was not at all what she had expected. The shaggy beard was a surprise, and she pictured his hair to be much shorter. His features were kind and caring, sympathetic and friendly, not stern or judgmental. As she observed his broken body, she realized he had been right; there *was* evil in the world masked as beauty. People who appeared kind and gentle could turn destructive. Great storms could change water to fire. And there was death. Mary, it seemed, had been misled.

She wondered if it should've been her limbless and on the ground.

"What can I do?" she asked, knowing there was nothing.

"Lift me up," he said dryly.

"I wish I could."

Mr. Lansly rode the tractor down the hill and raced along the gravel path. "Mary, continue to gather your information," he told her.

"But I already know. You were right."

The corner of the lift sliced the trunk of the oak tree as the tractor flew past. "No. There's more," he called to her. The tractor collided with the resting Jesus and pushed him along the ground. "I know there's more. Keep learning. There's more . . ."

"Wait!" Mr. Lansly released him, and Jesus slid along the slick mud of the bank. A massive splash erupted as he plunged into the water. He sank without screams or bubbles. "Jesus!" she called. "Can you hear me? Jesus!"

He did not respond. He was gone. Her son was gone.

12
ALICE

He slept in his hiding spot close to the sky. The ceiling provided him protection from the storm and its heavy winds, but the morning brought rays of hot sun that pounded the roof. When the heat became unbearable, he poked his head out from behind the corner of the rafter. "Good morning, Bluebell!" a chipper voice immediately greeted him. He pulled his head back in. "Come out, Bluebell. It will not be as terrible as you think. In fact, I believe you will find our time together to be quite agreeable." He tucked himself deeper, attempting to hide even from her voice. "You will never have to be concerned with finding shelter from storms, and there are always plenty of provisions from the church events."

Alice quieted as the Strange Man entered. He came into the empty church through the door behind the stage. He wore plainclothes: jeans and a light cotton shirt. There was urgency to his walk and a perplexed look to his face. He made his way to the aisle and knelt, staring intently at the cross. He then clasped his hands, closed his eyes and began to whisper. "Dear Lord, though I cannot completely or clearly understand your ways, I know that they are not without reason or purpose. I have just learned you have decided to take Audrey Lansly into your Kingdom. I will take solace in that, for she is now in your arms—perhaps the very arms she has so missed in the months following the loss of her mother."

In that instant, the heat seemed to rise even higher. Bluebell darted his head out again. He spread his wings and fanned them lightly. "Lord, please give me the strength this fine morning to comfort the troubled Mr. Lansly in his hour of need. Please watch over him as you have watched over each member of this church. Thank you, dear Lord. Amen."

Bluebell made himself visible by flying down onto one of the ceiling fans' still blades. "Alice, is it true what he says? About Audrey?"

"I am sorry, Bluebell, but it does sound that way. I was hoping this church would see more of the child. I quite liked her. Not many would have had the courage to remove a broom from the hands of Mrs. Stein as she. And she had an obvious affection towards you, which would have made her visits all the more delightful. It 'tis quite depressing, is it not?"

The Strange Man stood and headed for the back of the church. He grabbed his cap from the row of wooden coat hangers and reached for the tall double doors. Bluebell flew down to the first pew. "Alice," he said. "I'm sorry, but I must leave now more than ever. You see, my friends and I, we all cared for Audrey very much. And Mary will be especially upset now. I'll ask some mice to keep you company. And I'll try to visit when I can. But right now, it is *Mary* who needs me."

"*Mice!* I am not about to share my church with one more rodent!" she shot back. "And I can guarantee you, Bluebell, if you fly through those doors, there will be no more answers. There is so much more, plenty more, that you will never have the privilege of learning if you leave. So go on, Bluebell, and ponder the mysteries with Mary and those others. Spend another cold winter outside with them while they stay unfeeling of the temperatures, but do not come back here for answers!"

The Strange Man thrust open the doors and sunlight poured into the church. The rays fell upon Bluebell, causing his blue feathers to sparkle. He thought of Mary and of cold winters. He thought of Alice and her answers. He and Mary had waited so long for him to find a way inside; and there he was. Yet Alice revealed her insights had little to do with the humans. They came instead from her own observations and through her conversations with others. So according to Alice, he and Mary never really needed the church—never really needed *her* to begin with. Bluebell realized then he was being manipulated. There was no question Alice's insights could've provided fresh perspectives to him and his friends. But just as the humans didn't know any more than an animal or statue, Alice didn't know any more than Mary or himself. *Their* observations were just as valid as hers. So when the heavy doors began to slowly swing shut, Bluebell confidently lifted himself from the pew and zipped through the air.

"Bluebell! Come back!" she cried after him.

But he flew as fast as he could. He turned himself sideways to fit through the narrowing gap and sailed through the doors just before they clicked shut behind him. The Strange Man, heading for his car, was startled as Bluebell whizzed over his shoulder. He soared freely, appreciating the cool air on which he glided. "Poor Alice," he said to himself as he flew high above the pines. "Poor, lonely Alice."

13

MR. LANSLY

He flew towards the familiar opening in the forest. He had made the trip hundreds of times, but as he came over the trees, he immediately knew something was wrong. Jesus, who had always been the cemetery's beacon in the sky, was no longer there. And as he approached the hill, he noticed a path of fallen headstones that led from the top of the hill all the way to Mary, who stood out like a bright blue electric light. The landscape was scarred with massive tire tracks, the river bank was littered with piles of strange sacks, and one of the power lines had snapped loose from the wooden pole and lay along the river's edge. Surely, he thought, the storm couldn't have left *this* much destruction in its wake!

He dipped beneath the trees and sailed through the cemetery. It wasn't until then he noticed Mr. Lansly standing near Mary. He attempted to land discreetly in the oak, yet several branches had broken in the wind and wet tissue clung to much of the tree, so he surprised them both by brazenly landing on Mary's shoulder.

"Bluebell!" Mary shouted ecstatically. "How glad I am to see you! I've been so worried! I thought—well, I was beginning to think the worst."

"Mary, what happened here?" he asked, eyeing Mr. Lansly as he oddly shoveled dirt upon Mrs. Lansly's grave.

"Oh it was terrible." Her inside eyes widened as she recalled the horrible events for Bluebell. "Mr. Lansly and Audrey tried to stop the river from rising, but the storm—it was too strong. Poor Audrey. The ground gave way beneath her, and she fell into the river. And then the light from the sky struck the power line, and the power line struck the water. Oh Bluebell, she was in the water when it caught fire!"

"Then it has already passed," he assumed, thinking of the Strange Man's warning to the congregation.

"What has passed?"

"The great storm. The thunders, the lightnings, the earthquake."

"I suppose it has, but it has taken Audrey with it," she said full of hopelessness.

Bluebell lowered his head. "Yes," he affirmed. "I heard it from the Strange Man."

"Is that where you have been all this time? Listening to the Strange Man?"

"Yes, I was at the church," he confessed.

Mr. Lansly gave a curious look to the bird whistling a somber tune upon Mary's shoulder. Her blue robe matched its blue feathers—and instantly, he knew he was inside the drawing he had found in Audrey's room after returning from the hospital.

The hospital. He had waited until daybreak to take her. And even then, he drove slowly. He knew they would not be able to revive her, so he allowed the last moments he had with her body to linger. The moment he turned her over to the hospital staff, he knew it would become final. She would be taken from him forever, and he would then have to begin the painful process of separating her soul from her body.

They checked her vital signs right on the floor of the lobby. "What happened?" the doctor asked as he held her limp wrist and listened to her silent heart through his stethoscope.

"The storm. Lightning. The power line. It hit the water," he said around the lump in his throat.

"Electrocution," the doctor confirmed. The scattered families in the waiting room watched from their chairs, as if her body was too small, too delicate to crowd around. The doctor nodded to the nurse behind him, and together, they lifted her onto a stretcher and covered her with a sheet. He then placed his hand on Mr. Lansly's shoulder. "Go home and begin making funeral arrangements. I'm sorry." He dwelled on the doctor's words. Someone was saying *"I'm sorry"* to *him*. It was real.

The bluebird appeared to look past him, to the river in the distance. He too took a moment and glanced to the river. Even with all the rain, it had never risen much beyond the edge of the bank. Trying to shake that haunting thought, he once again concentrated on returning soil to his wife's grave. "Damn bird," he muttered.

"Mr. Lansly," Mary continued, her voice quivering, yet hushed as if to be sure he wouldn't hear her, "he turned—*evil*. He pushed Jesus from the hill with the tractor and rolled him into the river." Bluebell whistled uneasily as his eyes followed the deep tracks that led to the bank.

"He's gone," Mary went on. "I haven't been able to speak with him since. Do you know what that means? We can die too, Bluebell. Statues can die!"

"No Mary."

"And Audrey, she'll be like the others, underground forever. She'll be like Allen Pummel over there or Andrea Stacks down by the river. She'll be—like her mother. And we'll never see her again."

"But Mary, Audrey isn't dead. Jesus isn't either."

"But I saw these things happen myself. You must believe me!"

"Of course I believe you, but they're not dead."

"What is this talk, Bluebell? Oh I would love to, but I cannot ignore the fact that they're gone."

"I just wasn't *at* the church this time. I was *inside* the church," he revealed.

Mary was silent for a moment. Stunned. Bluebell had finally done it. It was the news she had been waiting to hear, what they had been working towards for so long. Yet the excitement of discovery just wasn't as satisfying as it had been before. How could she allow herself to feel excited in a time of such despair? Besides, after witnessing the death of Audrey and the destruction of Jesus, she began to wonder whether or not they should even continue to gather knowledge. She was afraid that their puzzle, once complete, would be no more than a hideous portrait—something that when seen as a whole, she would wish they had never begun to piece together. If death and destruction were commonplace, she figured they'd be better off not knowing the truth. "Oh?" she finally responded, fighting to tame her interest.

"I spoke with the other Mary," he added.

A spark shot through her, but somehow, she was still able to temper the excitement in her voice. "What was the Mary like?" she asked calmly.

"Her name was Alice."

"*Alice?* Why that's a strange name for a—" She stopped herself, knowing she had to keep an open mind. "I suppose Alice is a fine name. What was Alice like?"

"There were not others to keep her company."

"How thrilling for her then to be visited by such a colorful bird as you!"

He chirped out a dry laugh. "She was very lonely, Mary."

"Oh. How sad."

"She came from a place called England, where she was made. She has traveled all over different lands and has lived in many kinds of places."

"England? How fascinating! It sounds so far away. Is it another planet perhaps?"

"I don't think so. It's on the other side of an ocean."

Mary could no longer hold back her curiosity. It began to overwhelm her. "Bluebell, I'm so proud of you!" she burst. "Finally, we are lucky enough to have a friend inside the church, and one who comes from such a strange land!" He nodded with a sense of accomplishment and pride for pleasing Mary, even though he could not bring himself to tell her that Alice had denied further communication. "Have you learned much from her so far?"

"I have! I've learned about *stages.*"

"*Stages?*"

"It's what I wanted to tell you. You see, you're Mary, and you're a statue living in the Ruthsford cemetery. That's your stage. I'm Bluebell, and I'm a bird. That's my stage. That's all it means. And eventually, when we're ready, our souls will move us to the next stage."

"You mean we *do* have souls?"

"Yup!" he chirped in confirmation. "Only Alice called them *spirits*. So you see Mary, Audrey and Jesus aren't really dead."

"They're just in another stage?" she finished.

"Exactly!" Bluebell flapped his wings and climbed upon Mary's head. "You can go when you're ready!" he announced to all who would listen. The pines stood attentive. The leaves seemed to sway in his direction. "You can all go when you're ready!" he repeated.

Mary thought for a moment about what Bluebell was saying. While it was comforting to know that Audrey and Jesus would live on, their departure still saddened her just the same. "Bluebell?" He hopped back to her shoulder. "Will we ever see them again?"

"I suppose it's possible. We've all met in this stage, haven't we? Only if we *do* see them again, they would not be as they were."

"What do you mean?"

"Well, when you go to the next stage, you're—different. But whatever you become, it will be you just the same. Alice believes that when the stage you're in now is over, you can choose what your next stage will be."

"Utter nonsense!" Mrs. Grant interrupted, appearing near the oak tree. She kept her raspy voice low, even though Mr. Lansly had moved to the bank to load the sandbags back onto the pick-up. "Do you think I *chose* to be here? Believe me, nothing could be further from the truth."

"But Mrs. Grant, you must've not been ready to leave the stage you were in. You must've left too soon," Bluebell timidly suggested. "And you're just here now because you're waiting for—*something*."

"Is this what that church statue told you?" Bluebell nodded. "And you believe her?" He nodded again. Mrs. Grant looked as if she were sucking on a lemon. "Well now I'm convinced this *is* hell. I have a talking bird telling me I've left unresolved business while I was living. Yes, I do believe we've all wound up in hell."

"Mrs. Grant!" pleaded Mary. "Bluebell has brought us some much needed good news. Please don't spoil it!"

Mrs. Grant raised her hand. "Let me finish, dear," she scolded. "You know how I know we're in hell? I know because there's a river over there, and I can't drown myself in it." She hovered above the ground and plucked a leaf from the oak tree. "And if I fell out of this tree, I wouldn't even get a scratch. That's how I can tell. I can't leave. There *is* no escaping hell." Her cigarette appeared, and she stuck it in the corner of her mouth. "Another stage you say? Well, I'll tell you, you can't die twice. Believe me, I've tried."

"Believe us," said Gareth. "No matter how hard she's tried—"

"She's *still* here," finished Arthur.

She bared her teeth at them like an angry dog, and then turned back to Mary, fixing her perpetually uneven, deep red lipstick by dabbing the corners of her mouth with her fingertip. "Do you really want to know about the afterlife, deary?" she asked. "Well, I remember attending an ice cream social of all things with some women from the local Chamber of Commerce when the topic of death came up. Those gullible drones were practically put in a trance by Betty Monroe's moronic account of how she choked on a potato a few years before. Let me tell you, the ice cream melted as Betty dramatically recalled how, being near death, she entered a tunnel at the end of which was a white light. She had those women to the point of hyperventilation as she told them how the light came closer and then surrounded her."

"Yes!" said Bluebell. "Alice said there would be a soft light!"

"Well then someone forgot to turn it on for me because all I saw was black! And then just like that," she snapped her fingers, "I was here! No Bluebell, you start as dirt, and you end up as dirt."

"But Mrs. Grant, we have to keep up hope," said Mary. "*I'm* willing to believe Alice is right."

She placed her hands on her hips. "White lights and reincarnation, huh? Suit yourselves. Next I suppose you're going to speak of gods and devils? It's all such rubbish that shouldn't consume our minds."

"I don't know." Mary said pensively. "What did Alice have to say about God, Bluebell?"

Mrs. Grant threw her hands in the air. "I give up!"

"I almost forgot!" shouted Bluebell. "That's the most important thing I've learned. We never needed the church, Mary. We never needed humans to teach us about God, or why we're here, or the world around us—because they're just trying to figure it all out the same as us! Alice, she didn't come up with her ideas just by listening to the humans."

"So all anyone really knows is that God is the one who created us?" she whispered.

"That's right, Mary," Bluebell whispered back.

The idea seemed frightening to Mary, but also somewhat liberating. If it was true, it would mean that the world was full of possibilities, full of many interpretations that, right or wrong, demanded exploration.

She looked to Mr. Lansly still loading sandbags along the bank. He heaved one onto the pick-up and then leaned against its side to rest. He looked to his sore hands, and so did Mary. They were large and rough with calluses. He gently ran his fingers over each palm, soothing the rough skin. He then took a deep breath and looked to the sky a moment before resuming his work. Suddenly, Mary saw him with fresh eyes. "I never thought of it before," she said in wonder. "After all this time, I can't believe I hadn't thought of it!"

"Thought of what?" asked Bluebell.

Mr. Lansly's hands. They were the hands of creation. At one time, she had been a mere vision in his mind, and through his power, he was able to turn that vision into a reality. He gave birth to her in the shed. He had given her life. And that meant he had power over her. And power over Arthur, Gareth, and Jesus. "*God is the one who created us and God is the one who will destroy us,*" Jesus himself had said. And Mr. Lansly had shown he could create. And he had shown he could destroy his creations.

"Mr. Lansly, *he's* my God," declared Mary.

"But how can that be?" asked Bluebell. "Who is *Mr. Lansly's God* then?"

"Well," she thought. "Just because he's *my* God doesn't mean he's the *only* God." She was satisfied, for the time being, with that explanation. Satisfied that it was one of a great many possibilities. Bluebell's discovery had taught her that the complex puzzle she had been trying to solve was just *too* complex, and that it was actually not just *one* puzzle, but hundreds—or thousands of puzzles that she could *never* solve! Yet strangely, she was comforted by this thought—comforted by the vastness of the universe. Because of the limitless possibilities, she could finally be relieved from finding definitive answers to definitive questions. She could now mold her own interpretations while simply enjoying the wonder of the world around her.

"Mr. Lansly! Hello? Are you out here?" The voice came from the edge of the woods. He had heard it, but continued to load sandbags. Mary recognized the Strange Man as he made his way between the tombstones. She had seen him at almost every burial. His words seemed to make the humans only more upset. He pulled out a cloth and rubbed his glasses before looking in astonishment at the condition of the cemetery.

"Not that aging bastard again," sighed Mrs. Grant.

"Mrs. Grant! You shouldn't say that about the Strange Man. What has he done to you?" asked Mary.

"Oh he never liked me. That damn fool was so insistent on getting Frank and I to go to his church, he'd set bulletins and pamphlets on our doorstep every Sunday. One day, he left one entitled 'You Can't Take Your Riches to Heaven.' Well, Frank was compelled to respond with a letter aptly stating that if God had intended for us to be poor, he would've made us foolish churchgoing folks giving up half our possessions just to keep his collection plate full. Ha!" she slapped her knee. "I just don't think that preacher ever had a sense of humor! Frank closed his letter by informing him not to expect future church events to be sponsored by The Silver Dollar!"

"He's a bastard, and you're a battle-ax!" hollered Gareth.

"He's a preacher, and you're a prune!" Arthur promptly added.

"Excuse me, Mr. Lansly. I came as soon as you notified me," he said, carefully stepping over the sandbags. He acknowledged his presence by nodding, but did not break from his work. "I came to offer you my condolences in person.

I can only imagine how troubling this tragedy must be for you."

"Uh huh." He piled the bags with increased ferocity, not glancing to the priest.

Sensing his terseness, he rushed to the detailed matters of his visit. "The hospital called shortly after you had, and they're bringing her over to the church tomorrow. Let's see, that would make it a Thursday service."

"That'll be fine," he answered.

"You know, Mr. Lansly, the town is praying for you. It's times like this I try to remind myself of the Lord's compassion. He's here to heal your pain and watch over you. Although it may be unfathomable at this time, we must try to remember that the Lord had a plan for Audrey. And now, He's caring for her in the most magnificent way. He has brought her closer to Him. No more is she confined to the flesh. She's with the Lord, and they're together in peace."

"Is that so?"

The priest pulled down the rim of his glasses and scanned the cemetery behind them. "Forgive my bluntness, Mr. Lansly, but what happened here? What did all this?"

"The storm," he mumbled.

"Surely the storm couldn't have done *that*." He pointed to Mary, her blue robe. "Surely the storm didn't crumble those headstones or litter your tree. It couldn't have made those deep tracks, shatter the crypt's window or remove the earth from your wife's grave. *What did this?*"

Mr. Lansly faced him. His eyes burned red into the priest's. "I said it was the goddamned storm!"

The priest stepped backwards. "Well," he said timidly. "This ground should portray His glory. I trust it will be proper by the time of the burial."

Mr. Lansly dropped the sandbag he had just lifted. "Is *this* His glory?" he asked, raising his hands. He raced to the foot of the hill. "Look at this!" he shouted as he kicked over a tilted headstone kept upright only by the support of a small rock. "Look at all of this—death!" Both men gazed up the hill populated with headstones, which were silhouetted by the late morning sun. He staggered away from the priest and stood with one leg over his wife's grave, and the other over what would become Audrey's. "This is no place of glory," he said, exhausted.

"The cemetery used to be his pride," whispered Mary.

"That was before he realized what it truly is," Mrs. Grant replied.

He tried to leave the clearing in a hurry, but under Mr. Lansly's fiery stare, the rattled man stumbled over a fallen branch. "I should be getting back to the church," he said, scrambling to stand upright. "I'll have Judy call to work out further arrangements. Good day Mr. Lansly."

After clearing the sandbags, he made his way up the hill and shut himself in the shed. There, he spent most of his days throughout the month that followed. From time to time, he'd step outside to look down the hill to Mary, who stood as a constant reminder of where his wife and daughter lay beneath the earth.

14
THE AWAKENING

August gave way to September. Near the end of the
month, leaves began to pile up and fill the spaces
between the gravestones. Unlike previous years, the
Lanslys were not there to rake beneath the oak. Mary
desperately missed seeing the family, especially Audrey. She
watched the green leaves slowly turn shades of vibrant red and
orange before falling off the tree and collecting on the ground
before her. It was sad to watch what had provided her shade
throughout the spring and summer eventually shrivel and turn
brown. It was like saying goodbye to another friend. She did,
however, at least take some solace in the fact that she knew
she'd be there to greet next year's leaves in the spring.

Mary marveled at her own shadow in front of her. The
angle of the morning sun that time of year in conjunction
with the thinning leaves allowed rays of light to glow upon her
with little interference. It provided a rare glimpse of her
complete profile. Still, this more holistic portrait remained
ambiguous. It only prompted her to ponder her features,
which she had never seen. "What do I look like, Bluebell?" she
asked.

"You're beautiful, Mary," he answered without hesitation.

"No. What do I *look* like? What *makes* me beautiful?"

He leaned forward from her shoulder and cocked his head so he could peer at her face. "Well," he began, "your face is slender and smooth. Your cheekbones sit high on your face—just like Mrs. Lansly's did. And your nose—it's no bigger than an acorn!"

"What else?"

"Your eyes—they're open most of the way, and when the sun goes down in the afternoon, they sometimes sparkle. Your eyebrows arch, just a bit, into your forehead. They remind me of those tasty tent worms in the trees along the river!" Mary giggled. "And your lips," he continued "look like two peaks in the center and then curve downward, just slightly, towards the corners of your mouth, but you are not frowning. In fact, I have always thought you looked quite peaceful."

"And just what would a bird know about lips? You have a beak for Christ's sake," said Mrs. Grant, yawning as she materialized from her crypt. "Some things just have to be discussed woman to woman. Take my hair for instance—"

"Yeah, it should have been dyed before you died!" Gareth blurted.

Ignoring him, she slapped the top of her scalp with her open palm and smoothed her white hair forward. "Consider yourself lucky you don't have my hair. It's simply out of control. Why, you don't even *have* hair. What a blessing, my dear!"

"No hair?"

"Well, perhaps you might under that covering." She rose up to the platform and bent forward to get a better look at where Mary's forehead ended and her stone-carved head cover began.

"I wish I could see what I looked like, just once. Mrs. Grant, you saw yourself in mirrors when you were alive. And Bluebell has seen himself in window reflections. But Arthur, Gareth and I—we have no idea what we look like."

"Believe me, it would be no surprise to them, my dear, to see how nauseating they are."

"I have an idea!" sang Bluebell. Still stretching forward, he fell from Mary's shoulder in his excitement. He quickly found footing in a crease of her robe. "I'll be right back!" he said, before bolting off through the trees.

Mrs. Grant circled Mary, inspecting her while cupping her hand under her chin. "Be glad you're not human, Mary." She stopped in front of her and brought her hands to either side of her stone face. "Your face is smooth. You won't have to worry about cracks for decades. Look at *my* face, this skin!" She felt the grooves on her cheeks. "The cracks and wrinkles of time won't affect you the way they did me. No one wants to see an old decrepit fool staggering about, looking like the walking dead. No Mary, you'll stay sturdy. That is, unless Mr. Lansly has another urge to be asinine!"

Mary did not reply. She figured she had little control over her fate. If her theory was correct, and Mr. Lansly *was* her God, she knew that just like with Jesus, he could take her without notice. Protesting would be no use. Whatever he chose for her, she would have to accept.

"He's certainly up to *something*," said Mrs. Grant, glaring up the hill to the shed. "Honestly! He's been in there all night. Is he trying to set a record?" They all were curious about Mr. Lansly's long hours in his workshop. Mrs. Grant and Bluebell had even tried to catch a glimpse inside. But there were no windows. And seldom did he open the doors. Loud pounding and clanking would often emanate from the shed. And at night, Bluebell reported seeing sparks from under the door.

"He's making our replacements!" cried Arthur.

"We're sure of it!" worried Gareth.

While Mary's construction seemed to be impervious to decay, the gargoyles had a justifiable reason to fret. Peculiar cracks had developed on each of their bodies. The thin, yet noticeable hairline fractures ran from both sides of their mouths to where their frames were mounted to the crypt. The tiny fractures grew more and more visible over the course of September until they became bonafide cracks in the stone. Ever since Mrs. Grant had made the discovery, Arthur and Gareth became obsessed with the thought that Mr. Lansly's time in the shed was spent crafting new creatures to hang from the crypt.

"Oh you two are being paranoid fools," said Mrs. Grant. "Although," she sneered, "I suppose it is not an altogether unlikely assumption. You *have* seen better days. And need I remind you, you were both merely ghastly afterthoughts. Ornaments that I had never asked be added, mind you. This crypt was not constructed with your additional, shall I say— bulk—in mind." Her eyes bulged as she examined the crack along Gareth's torso. "And here I thought Mr. Lansly was a skilled craftsman. Ha!" The gargoyles moaned relentlessly in despair until Bluebell's return.

Finally, he flew into the cemetery gripping a piece of string with his toes. At the end of the string dangled an object that gave off bursts of bright light as it swayed back and forth capturing and then reflecting the sun. "A wind chime fell off the porch a while back. This piece is mirrored, Mary, so you should be able to see your reflection in it."

"How perfect, Bluebell! I know I can cast a shadow; I *must* be able to cast a reflection."

Bluebell flapped his wings and hovered as steadily as he could, allowing the glass to dangle in front of Mary. "Can you see?" he asked.

Mary squinted. Her blue robe swayed before her. "A little higher." As Bluebell adjusted the mirror, her neck and chin came into view. And then, for the very first time, she was able to see her own eyes. The statue staring back did not seem as if it was her at all, but a stranger's face she was forced to accept as her identity. It was the oddest sensation, exhilarating and surreal. Yet Mary hadn't a moment to process her mental and physical disconnect. Her moment of self-discovery was short-lived.

A familiar, yet unbearable sound came from the shed—a sound that made everyone's stomach churn uneasy: the tractor was trying to turn over. Startled, Bluebell flew erratically, and the mirror jostled before Mary. She desperately tried to keep focus, but all she could see were blurred reflections of the gravestones on the hill behind her and blinding flashes of the morning sun. When she finally looked away from the mirror, she was unable to see Bluebell directly in front of her. She could only see the streaks of sunlight that had burned into her eyes. Bluebell lost his grip and dropped the mirror. It shattered on the platform. "I can't see anything!" Mary panicked. "All I can see is—white light!"

The tractor growled to life. Black smoke poured out of the shed's door. They waited in fearful anticipation. Bluebell held his head low, peering in the direction of the hill while nervously stamping his feet upon Mary's shoulder. "That bastard wouldn't dare," said Mrs. Grant. She stood beside Mary with her arms folded.

"It's okay," Mary said, trying to be brave. "Let it be," her voice cracked. "If it is meant to happen, then we should just let it be."

"If he destroys Mary, next he'll come after us!" whined Gareth.

"He'll smash us into bits with his hammer and throw us in the river!" assumed Arthur.

"And if he destroys my crypt, I'll have nowhere to go," whispered Mrs. Grant.

The tractor roared out of the shed, and soon the machine appeared atop the hill like a snarling monster that had just escaped from its cage. Its rusted-red metal parted the foliage along the narrow path as it began to chug down the hill. Yet as it passed the trees and descended further into the clearing, Mary watched Mrs. Grant's face relax. She left Mary's side and instead peered from behind her crypt. Bluebell too relaxed his body. He lifted his head from his shoulders and scurried over Mary's head to sit on her opposite shoulder. The white light that blocked her vision finally began to dissipate just as the tractor came into her view, and then she too saw that the tractor was no longer a threat. It moved towards her just the same, but the lift was already occupied by a massive thing covered in a black tarp. She felt relief, and then a bit of guilt for feeling such relief. Yet perhaps, she figured, it simply wasn't her time to move onto the next stage.

The machine bobbed with each subtle bump and depression in its way. He moved the tractor forward slowly, careful not to shift the weight of the bulky cargo. He swiveled off the path and between headstones. He circled behind Mary and pulled up to her side. There, he finally halted. His beard was full. He scratched his skin through the thick dark whiskers as he lowered the lift. With her vision now in clear focus,

Mary eyed the peculiar thing he had angled towards her. As it became level with the ground, she realized the object, though large, was actually not quite as tall as her.

His eyes were red from lack of sleep, but he was more awake than ever as he jumped off the tractor. He took a moment to caress the tarp, feeling the solid curves beneath. He then rushed around the thing like a mad scientist, unhooking ropes and bungee cords. Grabbing hold of the tarp with both hands, he slowly pulled it forward until it fell in a dusty heap before his feet. He stood with his hands clasped behind his head. Even though it was his creation, seeing it in its intended destination in the cemetery, he was stunned with both marvel and tearful disbelief.

Mrs. Grant crept from behind the crypt with a look of pure astonishment. Bluebell whistled quietly. And Mary was simply speechless. The white stone shimmered with crystal deposits, making the new statue appear to be straight from heaven. It was in the image of a girl who stood with bare feet upon a circular platform. She seemed to be somewhat curious by the way she stood on her tiptoes, as if straining to hear an adult conversation. She wore a sundress, which met her legs at the knee. Her hands were locked in front of her, giving a touch of bashfulness to her pose. Her hair was loosely curled in delicate wisps of stone. And her lips, neither a smile nor frown, were in perfect balance. But it was her eyes that drew Mary's attention. Her pupils focused above her, locked in a child's eternal questioning stare. And the way the statue was positioned, that questioning gaze was placed directly upon Mary.

Mr. Lansly ran his hand along her cheek and curled his fingers under her chin. "Welcome, Audrey, to your new home." A rush of tears flooded his eyes, clouding his vision of his creation. He was painfully aware that the girl of stone who stood before him was not Audrey, and that she could not replace her.

It was during his time in the shed, where slowly, over hours of carving the magnificent statue, he finally and truly began to separate soul from body. He realized that to keep his daughter alive, to keep her real, he must do so through photographs, through songs they once sang together, through *memories*. The icon merely aided in the transition. It was a comfort to him, knowing that when reality became too much to bear, there would be a physical, permanent representation of the life his daughter once had.

He returned to the tractor and tilted the lift slightly forward before carefully reversing the tires. The huge stone slid into place, its position finalized. He admired her for a moment longer before returning the chugging machine to the shed.

"It is simply uncanny," said Mrs. Grant, stepping closer to examine the frozen girl. "It's almost, dare I say, *ghostly*." She circled the platform, critiquing the statue while holding her long cigarette to her side.

"It looks just like her," said Bluebell. He flew from Mary and landed on the other statue's shoulder. He pecked at the stone. "You're side-by-side now, Mary."

"It's Audrey!" declared Arthur.

"I *knew* she was alive!" Gareth shouted.

"That's not Audrey," Mary replied, unable to look away from the realistic carving. "It's just—a statue. Only stone." Mrs. Grant dropped her jaw, perturbed that Mary did not catch the irony of her own statement.

For a moment, all was silent as they looked upon the unmoving version of Audrey. The growling tractor had been secured in the shed. No birds chirped. The animals in the woods stood still. Even the surging river seemed to quiet and fade into the background. It was as if all the attention nature could muster was focused on the statue of Audrey. But then, just as soon as the stillness had come, a strong wind swept through the top of the oak. The gust shook the limbs and blew loose a fresh bundle of leaves in a shower of color. They fell as slow as snowflakes as they cascaded over Audrey, welcoming her.

"Mary, is that you?" a weak voice asked.

Shocked, Bluebell jumped from the statue's shoulder and flew back to Mary. Mrs. Grant stood steady between Mary and the statue of Audrey as the remaining leaves drifted through the air and fell through her translucent body. She brushed her hair from her ear and leaned towards the new statue, listening.

"*Audrey?*" Mary asked.

"Where am I?" she spoke again, her eyes adjusting to the bright light.

Mrs. Grant looked back and forth between the two, wondering if it could really be the same girl who had once played in the surrounding woods.

Mary fumbled for words. "You—you're in the cemetery."

"Your voice is so soft. I can hear your voice!" she realized. As her vision came into focus, she was welcomed by Mary's loving embrace. "I can see you clearer now. You look the same, but somehow, more clear." She looked to Bluebell sitting upon Mary's shoulder. "I'm glad to see Bluebell has made it home okay."

Bluebell slid down Mary's arms. "Thank you, Audrey," he nodded. "I'm very fine, especially now!"

"Bluebell! I can understand you! Your chirping, somehow it makes sense!"

"Of course it does, dear," said Mrs. Grant, satisfied it was in fact Audrey. "That's the great perk around here," she said with a touch of sarcasm.

Audrey could see the trees blowing in the distance, but did not feel the breeze. She could not move her limbs, but absent was the urge to adjust her position. She strained to see her body below. Although she could not, she knew what she had become. "How did I get like this?" she asked. "Why am I like this?"

No one offered an immediate answer, but Mary searched her thoughts. She looked to the river, to the trees and then back to her home among the monuments. "You may not realize it now," she said, pausing to look at Bluebell for reassurance, "but you *chose* to be here."

Audrey thought for a moment too. "I suppose I did," she said.

15
THE OTHER SIDE

black car made its way down the gravel path. "What now?" asked Mrs. Grant, annoyed, as she slipped behind Audrey.

As the car reached the bottom of the hill, Mr. Lansly appeared from the trail on the opposite side of the cemetery. "It's over here!" he yelled, running through the cemetery, waving to the driver of the elongated car.

"Another burial," said Bluebell.

"Just the one car?" asked Mary, curious. "No mourners?"

Mrs. Grant stomped her foot. "Oh of all days to be buried!"

Audrey strained to view the ground in front of her. She managed to see just the edge of a brown patch sewn into the earth. "Is that where *I'm* buried?" she asked.

"Yes," Mary answered.

"It's so strange. I'm underground, next to my mother."

"That's not you, Audrey. You're up here—with us now."

Mr. Lansly held up his hand, and the car halted. The tall driver stepped out and shook his hand. From the passenger side, emerged the Strange Man. Mr. Lansly clasped his hands and bowed slightly towards him before proudly pointing up the hill to the headstones. The fallen ones had been erected, the cracked ones replaced. "As you can see, I've been fixing up the place. I've gotten all the spray paint removed, except of course for the obvious." He nodded, and both men looked to Mary. He had only been able to remove one layer of the thick paint, so she remained a faded shade of blue. "But look *next* to Mary," he beamed. "She's my most wonderful creation yet. She'll be for the children—those who visit," he lowered his head, "and those buried here."

The priest patted his shoulder. "I'm glad to see you've regained your inspiration and dedication to this fine hallowed land."

"Oh I have! I'm planning to start on a new Jesus, even larger than the first! And I have many other restoration ideas in mind."

"Oh?"

"Colored lights to shine on the statues at night. Motion detectors to keep the teens away."

The priest smiled. "That sounds splendid. But right now we *do* have the lord's work to tend to."

"Of course. Of course we do." Mr. Lansly took a key out from his pocket, and the men followed him to the crypt. "You know, all of this is just more important when you have your own buried here." The priest nodded sympathetically. He removed the padlock from the crypt's door and tossed it to the grass. "Now if you two gentlemen will just help me push this door open, we can get your entombment underway."

A spark of fury erupted in Mrs. Grant. "Just what is going on I'd like to know!" she hollered. "They can't just barge into my home like that!" As the men heaved their weight against the rusted door, she began to charge towards the crypt.

"Mrs. Grant, no!" pleaded Mary.

"And why not, darling?" she said, spinning back towards Mary. "I've got a surprise for them when they finally *do* get that door open. You're about to see what three men experiencing a heart attack look like!" She floated towards them with a flagrant disregard for being noticed. Her arms extended in front of her, reaching towards the men with her fingers positioned in tense claws, ready to gouge the trespassers. If they had turned around at that moment, they would've seen her pale skin, her bright jewels sparkling in the sun, and her teeth clenched in anger. She rounded the back of the crypt and dissolved inside, waiting for the right moment to unleash her terror.

But before she could be given the satisfaction, the men were startled by a sudden loud bang behind them. They quickly spun to see the rear door of the hearse had mistakably flopped open. The abrupt jolt caused the car to bounce up and down. Mr. Lansly chuckled as the three regained their composure. "Have spooks in your graveyard?" the driver joked.

As if to answer his question, Mrs. Grant immediately shrieked, "And just what the hell are you doing here!" Her voice echoed throughout the cemetery, above the trees and across the river.

"Well hello to you too, my dear!" a man's voice promptly replied. The startled men looked to locate the mysterious voices. Bluebell flew to an outer limb of the oak to do the same.

Suddenly, Mrs. Grant materialized beneath the oak. She marched towards Mary and Audrey. Behind her, she dragged a peculiar-looking elderly man by his sleeve. He fumbled after her, madly pressing his cane into the ground to keep up. When she finally halted beside Mary, the man took a moment to adjust himself. He brushed the dust from his sleeves, straightened his suit coat by tugging at its corners and repositioned his top hat. When he was satisfied, he pressed his shiny black cane back to the ground and stood with his shoulders back and his head held high. He was shorter than Mrs. Grant, and with his oversized black suit, tall hat and cane, he looked like a tiny magician.

"Just what are you doing in *my* cemetery?"

"*Your* cemetery? I'll have you know I picked this place out myself. Paid top dollar for it, I did."

Mrs. Grant folded her arms and frowned. "You look ridiculous in that hat. No one wears those anymore."

"And what is it *you're* wearing, Loretta?"

"You should know! You stuffed my corpse in it for the funeral."

"Ah yes. I almost forgot. As I recall, it was an original I had shipped from Paris," he said proudly.

"Well obviously they hung the rotten thing out the window on the ride over." She lifted the dress off her shoulders and let it drop. The jagged fabric along the bottom of the purple gown swayed from side to side.

"One minute back with you, and I need a martini," he declared.

"Oh you and your alcohol! I never could stand that about you, you know."

"I've always said a good martini helps keep the headaches away."

"Who *is* this guy?" asked Arthur.

"Who cares? I like him already," cracked Gareth.

"Haven't we seen him somewhere before?"

"Not around these parts," Gareth giggled.

"Who said that!" Mr. Grant lifted his shoulders to his ears and looked about the cemetery.

"Oh never mind! Here's your martini!" He happily took the glass that had materialized in her hand. He extended his pinky while enjoying a long sip, and then finished with a satisfied sigh.

"Well at least come over here so Mr. Lansly doesn't see us." She led him again by his sleeve, and they hid within Audrey's shadow. They watched as across the cemetery, Mr. Lansly helped the driver and the priest lift the coffin inside the crypt.

"Why is your body here, Frank?"

"Why do you think, Loretta? I'm here because I'm dead of course!"

"Yes. Yes. But what I don't understand is why you weren't buried next to your second—or is it *third* wife by now—Frank? Well I suppose I *can* understand it. She didn't *want* you buried next to her? Or maybe you were exhumed for bad behavior?"

"Loretta, I was seventy-five years old when you died. Now who would have married me? And darling, did you fail to notice there is enough room for *two* of us in that crypt?"

"Well I always figured that was just a ruse to show those Chamber of Commerce phonies that you were an upstanding citizen, all the while hiding your true intentions of leaving me here to rot alone." She turned her back for just a moment before promptly spinning to face him again. "So there is no second wife you say, huh? Then why couldn't you even bother to visit?"

"I just—I just couldn't bear to, darling." Using his cane to keep his balance, he knelt before her. "Not after knowing you killed yourself because of me. That's why I sold it."

"Sold what?" she fumed.

"The Silver Dollar—put it up for sale the day after your funeral, I did. I gave up on the idea of expanding it into a chain, and instead sold it at a loss. You know me, I never wanted to go out on the bottom, but I just couldn't go through with the plans." He held out his hand to her. "With you gone, I was lost. I didn't have that special fight in me anymore. You know, that spark that you bring out in me so easily," he said with a light chuckle. "I should have retired in my sixties like you had asked. I realized that only when I was alone, old and tired, full of regret. All I had to look forward to my last few years was passing on—and the possibility of seeing you again."

For the first time Mary had ever noticed, Mrs. Grant's lips twitched upward in a smile. She wrapped her fingers around the top of his cane. "Oh Frank," she said, pulling his head to her in a light hug. "Now this doesn't mean I forgive you," she assured him. "Playing second fiddle to a lousy restaurant is nothing a wife should have to put up with. But I *am* willing to admit the whole suicide ordeal may have been a bit drastic."

"Wait a minute," Mary interrupted. "The story—it *was* made up then. If he just died, then you *couldn't* have murdered him!" Mr. Grant looked to Mary and began to realize the cemetery was much more than what it seemed.

"*Murder!*" she bellowed. "Who said anything about *murder?* Suicide, yes. But murder I'm not into."

She helped her husband stand. They watched as the hearse moved back up the hill and as Mr. Lansly returned the padlock to the crypt door, finalizing the new arrangement. "So we fought like hell, and now we're both finally here," she sighed.

"But we're here together," he added.

As Mr. Lansly headed for the house, the couple stepped out from the shadows and surveyed the land. "Loretta, do you see those two gargoyles on our crypt?" he asked.

"*See* them? I have to deal with those wretched creatures on a daily basis!"

"Well it was *I* who designed them."

"*You?*"

He nodded proudly. "With the help of that caretaker fellow, that is. I suggested they resemble cats. I knew how much you loved them. What were their names? Fizzer and Fuzzball?"

"Fuzzer and Finley," she corrected.

"Well regardless, pretty clever if you ask me."

"Do you mean to tell me that those two are supposed to be my beauties?"

"I thought you would have adored the idea."

"I don't believe it!" she seethed. She disappeared only to reappear below Arthur and Gareth. "To think you two beasts were modeled after my babies! Ha!" She looked up to them and shook her head in disgust. "Not even in the ballpark. Not even on the same planet," she complained.

"Well," said Gareth, "actually, we've been meaning to tell you something."

"Yeah. We've been waiting for the right moment," Arthur added with apprehension.

She impatiently chewed the corner of her mouth. "Well? *Speak* you wicked little monsters."

"We *are* Fuzzer and Finley," Gareth revealed. "Only we were *never* Fuzzer and Finely," he explained. "We were always— Arthur and Gareth."

Mrs. Grant's jaw dropped. "I don't believe it!"

"We were going to tell you," promised Arthur. "Honest!"

"But we figured as long as you didn't know, we could be ourselves."

"Yeah, we didn't have to behave!"

"We didn't have to be nice!"

"And we could have more fun!"

"*Fun?* You call abusing an old lady *fun?*" She placed her hands on her hips and studied their faces. "Are you *sure* you're Fuzzer and Finley?"

"As sure as I remember throwing up on your green shag carpeting," Gareth quipped.

"You *are* my two babies!" she gushed. "I've missed you all this time. And all this time here you were right with me!" She levitated to them and promptly kissed and nuzzled their gothic faces. The gargoyles gagged and screamed, and Mrs. Grant immediately dropped back to the ground, frowning in disappointment. "And to think I had you two in the same bed as me, trying to steal my breath away in the middle of the night so I'd suffocate to death, no doubt!"

"I don't feel so good," said Gareth.

"Me either. I'm feeling queasy," added Arthur.

"And how do you think *I* feel, being deceived all this time?" She turned to her husband in a pout. "Oh, look what a menace you've caused!"

But when Mrs. Grant turned back to the gargoyles, she brought her hand to her mouth in a horrified gasp. The fractures that ran along their bodies began to widen spontaneously. And with a deep rumble, the growing cracks shook loose their teeth and sent their horns crashing to the cement walkway. "This is it!" cried Gareth.

"We're goners!" Arthur shrieked just before his mouth broke away from his face.

Mr. Grant clutched his wife as they watched the gargoyles' faces crumble. Their bodies ripped apart from the crypt's structure and collapsed amid a powdery mist. Mrs. Grant lifted her dress and tiptoed aside to allow the remains to roll to the grass. The group stood in silence as the dust lingered over the ground like a low fog.

"So sudden," Audrey said, finally breaking the stunned silence. "What caused it to happen so suddenly?"

"I don't know," Mary answered in distress. "Bluebell?" She hoped he would be able to offer an explanation, but he could not. Instead, he looked to where the gargoyles had collapsed and then to Mrs. Grant.

"Don't look at me like that, Bluebell," she said. "I didn't do anything. I never wanted *this* to happen. This is just terrible!" She walked in a circle, panicking. "Just terrible!"

Bluebell flew into the settling dust to examine what remained of the gargoyles. He pecked at a piece of broken marble. "I'm not sure *what* would cause this," he called back. And just as he was about to lift from the ground, he found himself unable to avoid a set of sharp claws that batted at him through the smoke. Luckily for Bluebell, the ghostly paw passed right through him. He flew swiftly to the oak tree as the calico and tabby crawled out from their broken encasements. Having failed to capture Bluebell, Arthur pounced on Gareth's tail, and Gareth chased Arthur between headstones.

Mrs. Grant watched in delight as her two cats tumbled and played freely in the grass. "How was I supposed to know your real names were Arthur and Gareth?" she called after them and then cackled. Mrs. Grant looked to her husband, and he to her. They joined hands and faced the river. Together, they walked into the morning with the cats, Arthur and Gareth, following close behind. Mary, Audrey and Bluebell watched as they slowly faded against the pines.

"Where did they go, Mary?" Audrey asked.

"They were ready," she answered simply.

"Are *you* ready, Mary?"

Mary wondered if in fact she was. "I don't know," she replied. "But don't worry, Audrey. I'll stay with you until *you're* ready."

APPENDICES

The Lanslys

Richard Lansly and Patricia Buchanan met while attending an art college in Northern Michigan. He studied sculpture and woodworking, while she majored in drawing and painting. The two became fast friends, which eventually led to a serious relationship. Both were athletic and shared a love of the outdoors. They would often take trips together—hiking, mountain climbing; and once had even climbed a glacier on Mount Rainier in Washington.

Upon graduating, Patricia soon became a moderately successful illustrator of children's books. Richard, frustrated and disillusioned with his lack of success in the art world, took a job at a small print house as a printing machine operator. Patricia encouraged him to continue his art on the side; and the two rented a small studio where both could work. Soon, much to his delight, his sculptures and carvings began to sell in local galleries and gift shops.

One day, an admirer of his work contacted him with a curious request—to design and create a tombstone for her late husband. Richard took the task seriously and created an ornate stone carving that captured her husband's love of the forest, complete with leaves, acorns and a perching squirrel. The design was such a success that other orders for tombstones quickly followed.

Richard and Patricia were married in 1978, and shortly thereafter received a call from officials in the nearby small town of Ruthsford. It was explained the town had been operating the local cemetery, and in recent years, it had fallen into disrepair due to lack of staff and interest in the burial ground. The town was looking to privatize the land. The purchase fees would be waived, and the deal would include the income from the amounts due on new and existing burial plots. To sweeten the deal, the officials pointed out that Richard could create and sell his ornaments and tombstones to the families of the deceased.

The Lanslys first balked at the proposition, finding it incredibly morbid. Yet after visiting the site, both fell in love with the land's secluded beauty. They built a house in the forest not far from the cemetery and then began the task of repairing the monuments and tending to the grounds. Richard took special pride in the land—and in the new creations he had made to adorn it.

At the end of that first summer, Patricia announced she was pregnant. They named their daughter Audrey, after Patricia's grandmother. The Lanslys vowed they would bring up Audrey different from how their parents raised them. They would provide for her an environment that was not restricting, but would instead allow her to explore and be creative. Audrey flourished in this setting, and took a liking to many different forms of art early on. As she got older, she especially enjoyed collage and producing her own homemade video productions.

When Audrey turned ten, Patricia was diagnosed with lymphoma. Not wanting to cause her family any worry, she kept the news from her daughter, and even her husband, until she began treatment for the cancer. Even during the treatment, she disguised her pain and fatigue with her smiles, never sharing her doctor's estimate on her low chances of survival.

Mrs. Loretta Grant (1911 – 1983)

Born to the founding mayor of Ruthsford, Loretta Horowitz lived a privileged childhood. Ruthsford, then and now, was primarily a farming community. And being the mayor's daughter, Loretta was one of the few children who did not have to help her family with farming chores, such as picking beans and cucumbers or tending to farm animals. Neither did she have household chores, of which most girls of her era had plenty. Instead, her time was spent taking private piano lessons and attending a prestigious ballet school outside of town.

Yet despite her privilege (or perhaps because of it), Loretta was incredibly lonely. Other children wouldn't invite her over to play. And even at her own eighth birthday party, the other children left her to open presents alone while they explored her family's mansion playing a game of hide-and-seek.

From then on, Loretta vowed never to become close to others since others seemed to distance themselves from her. Her friends instead became the family's housecats. Reluctantly, they allowed Loretta to dress them in doll clothes, complete with bonnets and jewelry.

When she was sixteen, she attended a campaign fundraiser for her father. There, she met Frank Grant, the son of a successful hardware store owner. Like his father, Frank had dreams of becoming a successful businessman. He took an immediate liking to Loretta, despite her initial indifference to him. But Frank persisted, calling her his "spark." By the time Loretta was twenty, she finally agreed to marry him.

Much to her disappointment, Frank fell short of his aspirations by not immediately materializing into the breadwinner she'd hoped. He invested in a string of failed business attempts, including farm equipment sales and a poorly-stocked mercantile store. They lived in a small house on the outskirts of town. And for the first time, Loretta found herself performing menial tasks, such as cooking, housecleaning and laundry.

In the spring of 1943, Frank had the idea to open a restaurant. Feeling it was time she had more of a say in his business ventures, Loretta selected the site and took over much of the planning and design. The end result was *The Silver Dollar*. Catering to all of Ruthsford and beyond, it was the first upscale restaurant in the area, featuring premium steaks and a flaming crème brûlée on the dessert menu. Loretta managed the staff and was known as a strict boss. Behind her back, workers would often imitate her barking orders between taking long drags on her thin cigarettes.

When asked why she simply didn't hire a manager, she snapped, "Because I need to keep an eye on my husband. We have to pay for all those martinis he guzzles down, you know."

With Loretta being a silent atheist, the Grants rarely attended church, yet donated to church causes regularly in order to maintain good faith in the town. This, however, did not stop the priest from continually requesting their presence.

Even though it was Loretta who was instrumental in the initial success of the restaurant, it became Frank's obsession. Working around the clock, he impressed even her with his ability to turn a profit. The couple soon became the wealthiest in all of Ruthsford. Yet despite the success of the business,

Loretta began to tire of its demands. She also began to resent Frank's exorbitant amount of attention given to it, rather than to his wife. She dreamed of moving to a larger city. She dreamed of traveling abroad. But as the years slipped by, she realized those dreams grew more and more unlikely. The Silver Dollar kept her stuck in Ruthsford.

She finally saw hope in their pending retirements. Yet when the time came, Frank could not bear to give up ownership and continued working, leaving Loretta alone in their large estate. Those familiar feelings of being left out as a child began to creep forward, and their marriage began to deteriorate. She filled the void by inviting inside two stray cats she had been feeding on the back porch. She named them Fuzzer and Finley, and doted after the felines as she had her family's cats in her childhood.

Life took an even more sour turn for Loretta when Frank, at the age of seventy-five, decided to expand The Silver Dollar into a chain. Around the time Frank's questionable business decision threatened to ruin them financially, Fuzzer and Finley both died within days of each other. To make matters worse, she later discovered from a posting at the grocery store that there was a recall on the brand of canned tuna she had fed the cats.

Loretta, distraught over the state of her marriage and death of her beloved felines, reasoned there was nothing left to live for. In 1983, at the age of seventy-two, she committed suicide in her Ruthsford mansion. The suicide was something of a legend in the small town, complete with various rumors and stories surrounding the circumstances. Some have even said her restless ghost can be seen wandering the Ruthsford cemetery near the crypt where her body is entombed.

Bluebell

Before Bluebell had hatched, a raccoon hungry for a meal attempted to invade his family's nest. His mother, desperate to protect her precious eggs, managed to scare off the animal—but sadly, suffered damaging attacks from its sharp claws. Upon returning to the nest, his father made the horrifying discovery that his wife had been savagely attacked and killed. Several days later, their children began to peck their way out of their shells. He was overcome by his loss, yet vowed to feed and care for their hatchlings as she would have done.

When it came time to leave the nest, Bluebell, the smallest of his brothers and sisters, did not travel far. He settled in an old wooden fence along the main entrance to the Ruthsford town cemetery, about a mile away from his childhood nest.

A timid bird by nature, he rarely traveled far from his home. Yet one winter day, when food was scarce, he began to search for berries in the forest on the other side of the two-track. He soon came upon a clearing and was immediately enchanted by its collection of tombstones and statues. To him, the statues looked as if they had been alive at one time and had merely frozen still in the wintery landscape. He discovered there was a river at the edge of the clearing and was excited to have found a continuous source of fresh water. Thirsty, he flew to its bank and drank from an opening in the ice. Upon his return, he flew past the statue of a beautiful woman and heard a voice say, "Hello bluebird!"

Startled, yet curious, he circled back past the woman and landed atop the tombstone in front of her. "Did you say something?" he asked with his head tucked between his shoulders.

"If you are looking for berries, there is a bush the other birds speak of along the path to the Lansly's house."

He tossed his head from side to side while coming to the realization that the frozen woman was in fact speaking to him. "Thank you. But who are the Lanslys?"

"They take care of us," she stated simply.

"Forgive me for asking—but *what are you?*"

"I don't know," she answered solemnly. "All I know for sure is that my name is Mary. What is your name?"

"I—I don't have a name," he confessed.

"Well you have the most beautiful blue feathers. I could not help but notice them against the white snow as soon as you flew over my shoulder. Blue happens to be my favorite color. Wait a moment—it just came to me!" she exclaimed. "What about *Bluebell?*"

"What is a *Bluebell?*"

"*You* are Bluebell! What do you think of that for your name?"

He needn't a moment to think before flapping his wings in delight. "My name is Bluebell!" he whistled ecstatically. "I have a name!"

From that moment on, Bluebell and Mary became best friends. He vowed to help her discover her origin and bring her information about the world outside her view. Their bond was so strong that when a group of teenagers threatened to desecrate Mary, he risked his own life to deter the vandals.

St. Mary's Catholic Church

One of the first buildings to be erected shortly after Ruthsford became an official town in 1907 was St. Mary's Catholic Church. The interior is filled with ornately-carved oak walls and tall wooden beams that support the high ceiling. The exterior was constructed almost entirely out of limestone extracted from a nearby quarry. In fact, it is for this reason of convenience only that the church sits on the outskirts of town instead of along the main road. Due to the heavy clay in the soil, the limestone absorbed a deep tan color. Cut into large plates, pieces of the rock jut out from the building, resembling tiny steps that lead to the top of the steeple. The tall steeple acts as a guide to visitors making their way from the center of town through the series of dusty dirt roads.

Father Donald Patrick presided over the congregation from 1968 until his retirement in 1999. Inspired in his youth by the charisma of black preachers, his deep, sometimes booming voice and energetic readings of the scripture cemented him as an irreplaceable member of the Ruthsford community.

Father Patrick had always been troubled by the lack of religious icons in the church, so on a pilgrimage to Europe in 1972, he used his own funds to ship a small bust of the Virgin Mary back to Ruthsford. The statue, he was told, was commissioned to be destroyed due to the renovation of the open square in which it was displayed. He placed it upon a modest pillar at the front of the church and enjoyed the many compliments it received. Many commented on how The Virgin Mary's light-blue headdress brought a welcome touch of color to the church.

Stephen Stromp lives in Michigan. He is also the author of *Where the Cats Will Not Follow* and *In the Graveyard Antemortem*.

Connect with Stephen Stromp
Join Email List: eepurl.com/caHNZT
Website: stephenstromp.com
Facebook: facebook.com/StephenStromp

Books primarily rely on word of mouth to find their way to readers. The best way to help spread the word about books like *Cracking Grace* is to leave a brief review on your favorite review site, such as Amazon.